The Idle Years

ISBN   : 975-92758-3-X
PRESS : Matsan

Editor   : Denise Mcqueen

Orhan Kemal Culture Center
Phone   : 90 (212) 292 92 45
Fax   : 90 (212) 293 63 39
Http   : //www.orhankemal.com
            www.orhankemal.org

The original title of this translated work is "AVARE
YILLAR".

ANATOLIA PUBLISHING
Address : Akarsu Caddesi No: 32, Cihangir,
            34433 Istanbul, Turkey
Fax   : 90 (212) 293 63 39
Http   : //www.anatoliapublishing.com

Orhan Kemal

The Idle Years

A novel

Translated by Cengiz Lugal

ORHAN KEMAL
15/09/1914 – 02/06/1970

His real name was Mehmet Raşit Öğütçü. Born in Adana in 1914, his father became a Member of Parliament in the first session of the Turkish National Assembly, and founded the "Popular Party" in 1930. The consequences of his political activities led the family to emigrate to Syria, leaving their son unable to complete his secondary education. These events are covered in his semi-autobiographical novel "My Father's House" (1949), which he prefaced as being the diaries of "A Nobody".

He later returned to the town of his birth and worked in a variety of jobs in cotton factories, and as a clerk at the Fight Against Tuberculosis Foundation. This period of his life, including his marriage to the daughter of a Yugoslav immigrant in 1937, became the subject of four future novels.

During his military services in 1939 he was sentenced to 5 years' imprisonment for his political stance. His time with Nazım Hikmet in the Bursa State Prison had an important influence on his socialist views. His memoirs of this period have also been published in book form. He moved to Istanbul in 1951, where he started to write full-time for a living.

His works often revolve around ordinary people struggling to make a living. Inspired initially by his own experiences in the 1930's, he went on to explore various subjects with his writing: The problems of farm and factory workers, the alienation of migrant workers in the big city, the lives of prison inmates, blind devotion to duty, child poverty, and the repression and exploitation of women. He has written 38 books (28 novels and 10 story books), some of which have been filmed or turned into plays.

In his works, he is never the aloof observer; in an effort to encourage people to achieve more in their lives, he utilises a realism that is both cautionary and instructive.

He died in Sophia in 1970, and is buried in Istanbul.

INTRODUCTION

The master of Realist Turkish Literature, Orhan Kemal, has hitherto only been published in Turkish. With the valuable contribution of the Turkish Minister of Culture, Mr. İstemihan Talay, we are now for the first time able to present the English translations of these works.

These English translations of the works of Orhan Kemal, Turkey's bestselling author, provide us with an important opportunity to open and introduce the Turkish culture to the world. Even though he is widely read and appreciated in Turkey, it would nonetheless be particularly satisfying for those of us involved in this work for his books to also be widely read and appreciated around the world.

We would like to take this opportunity to thank the Turkish Minister of Culture, Mr. İstemihan Talay, for his work and contribution in enabling a large foreign readership to access Turkish literature in general and Orhan Kemal in particular, and thereby introducing Turkish cultural values to a wider audience.

Orhan Kemal Culture Centre
Işık Öğütçü

I

After Yorgi married his cousin and closed down the bran shop, our football team disbanded. Gazi and I went over to a different club, and naturally took Hasan Hussein with us.

I was good at taking penalties, and Gazi's headers were wonderful. And unless something was related to football, we had no time for it. However Hasan Hussein, in spite of his shabby appearance in his aging, frayed jacket, stubbornly retained his ties with school so that he might one day become an accountant, and be able to afford plenty of lamb chops.

We hung out at a café known as "the Cretan's".

The café stood in the shade of large eucalyptus trees, and was a perfectly uniform rectangular shape, with rows of windows on each side. It was quite a distance away from the city centre. Gentlemen who had had enough of the rumble of the city would come out here, place a chair under the shadow of its eucalyptus trees, and silently meditate, particularly when the weather was nice.

The owner of the café was actually from Crete. Although he was much older than we were, he was a lively and entertaining host. He'd speak a broken Turkish with a heavy accent, and sell hash to some of his less savoury punters.

I'd leave home every morning, pretending to be off to school, with my books tucked under my arm, my yellow-striped school cap on my head, I'd head off to the Cretan's. I'd wait for Gazi and Hasan Hussein at the crossroads. If they arrived first I'd inevitably get grilled about my tardiness. They would have a little go at me, but then we'd all be laughing and chatting together, absent-mindedly throwing stones at passing strays, admiring the sparkling taxis gliding over the shiny tarmac, and slowly making our way to the café. The proprietor would usually still be snoring in bed. Not wanting to wake him up, we'd quietly sneak in, light the stove, put on the kettle to brew the tea, and pop over to the grocers next door to get some shelled walnuts and fresh bread.

"Well done," the Cretan would say, when he woke to find everything on the go, "Good on you, lads!"

Occasionally he'd come out with some incredible piece of news. For example:

"I was just about to go to bed," he'd say, "and this car pulled up. Four or five people got out, went inside the house over there, then the car drove off. The people are still in there!"

We all panicked at this news. What if those people had come over to arrange our marriages? What if the girls' old man said yes?

You see, we had become lovers with the girls from the red-tiled house. The house was set in a wheat field across the road, facing the café. Three girls lived there, and the eldest was going out with the owner of the café. Mine was the middle one, and the youngest was going out with Gazi. Hasan Hussein didn't have anyone. That's because Hasan Hussein had no intention of having anything but the best. He was saving himself to marry a girl from either a very rich or a very well known family.

Although he was saving himself, and refusing to take on a lover even on a temporary basis, Hasan Hussein still bunked off school to be with us. And back in those days, when we beat up other guys for making impertinent remarks about our girlfriends, he would be the first to wade in, hitting harder than anybody. On windy nights, when we would sometimes have to wait for the girls under the old sycamore tree for hours, he would wait by our side. Not once did he ask, "What am I doing here? What's this got to do with me?" During the hours when we all separated out to shelter under different trees, thinking only of love and making love, he would stay over in the orange grove, some twenty metres away, pacing up and down in a steady rhythm, smoking, coughing intermittently, and now and then taking out his glass eye and wiping it on his handkerchief.

My girlfriend did wonder about this.

"Patient and loyal, isn't he?" she asked.

"What, because he's waiting there?"

"Mmm, yes, because he's waiting there... But also because he's not getting himself a girlfriend..."

We would signal the girls from under the old sycamore with a lit match, and anxiously wait for the reply from the sofa by their window, which they gave using a lantern. We would sometimes be waiting for ages. Then, as we stood under the trees in the wet night, the skies rumbling, lightning flashing, and the harsh wind breaking up on the dry branches around us, the girls would eventually come running towards us, emerging from the darkness like nervously flickering ghosts. Mine would rub her hands in a repetitive, nervous way, then grab hold of my hand and hold it to her chest:

"Look, feel that heartbeat! If I drop dead one of these days, it'll be your fault!"

One of the others might hear her. "If only they appreciated what we do for them..." she'd whisper.

One night, when they'd managed to get their father off to bed, and told their mother they were just popping over to their neighbour's, they were just tiptoeing down the stairs, when one of them stepped on the cat! The huge squeal made their old man leap out of bed. All our arrangements nearly went down the drain that night...

Once they were with us, each of us would take our loved one by the hand and wander across the slippery damp earth in a different direction while Hasan Hussein stayed behind, lighting himself a cigarette and starting to cough hoarsely.

We made a new friend one day. This new friend of ours had dark eyes and a shrivelled white face, always made us laugh out loud, and consistently beat us all at backgammon without losing a single point. He, Nejip, was from Istanbul and was here doing his military service.

Nejip was getting his discharge papers soon, and he couldn't stop telling us all about Istanbul. The marvellous picture he painted played on my childhood memories, making Istanbul a bright land of promise. It made my home town seem lacklustre by comparison.

"Around here," he would say, "you could have all the talent in the world and not get anywhere. You should come over to Istanbul and see what a real city is like! There was this guy Ali, working at the tobacconists. From Sinop, he was. When he first started playing football, he wasn't even as good as you guys. Now he plays inside-left for Fenerbahce!"

One day Gazi said, "What do you say? Shall we just up and go?"

"What about our girlfriends?"

"Don't worry about them... There's no shortage of girls in Istanbul."

"What about my school?" I asked.

"What about it?"

"Well, you know..."

Gazi looked dubious.

"What're you looking like that for, Gazi?"

"As if you were going to school..."

"Alright... But what about the fares to get there?"

"Getting there... That's a point. Let's say we somehow got hold of boarding passes from Mersin..."

"What would we eat on the way? Let's say we arrive in Istanbul. Where would we stay? How would we feed ourselves?"

"Hang on," said Gazi, "let's find Reshat and Ahmet. They can teach us how to work the looms, and we can work for a while in the cloth factory and save up some money..."

"Yeah, then we can up and go. Weaving would be a worthwhile trade in Istanbul too. If we find ourselves a bit short..."

"If we found ourselves a bit short, we'd do whatever

work came our way…"

"Of course we would. Hasan Hussein probably wouldn't want to get his hands dirty, but…"

"Don't think about Hasan Hussein. Remember what Nejip said? About that guy Ali from Sinop, who worked in the tobacconists? Remember? Who knows what we could do?"

"Maybe, maybe… If we could get some decent training. But let's not tell Hasan Hussein… If we're looking at Fenerbahce first, we might make the national team eventually, eh?"

"Why not? It's perfectly possible."

All our conversations now centred on Istanbul.

We decided to start working at the factory.

Later, we told our girlfriends of our decision to go to Istanbul. We painted such a marvellous picture that the girls, who were a few years younger than us, got as excited as we were. They suggested that we all go together. We could all go, work, save up, and go to the movies every Sunday. We'd have children, and we'd educate them and raise them to be decent people. Naturally we'd age, and grow old together… Until death do us part, all under one roof…

Gazi's girlfriend clapped her hands together.

"Oh, oh! It would be wonderful! Wonderful!"

"Let's not wait," suggested mine, "let's go now!"

Yeah, now we'd seen a horseshoe, all we needed was three more horseshoes and a horse, and we'd be there!

The next day, we went and found Reshat and Ahmet, the weavers. Reshat and Ahmet were brothers, and both had complexions as white as paper. We knew each other from Yorgi's bran shop, and they were huge football fans too. They'd been working on the looms in the factory for years. They'd always turn up to play football bleary-eyed, and covered in cotton. They were surprised to see us at the factory. Ahmet listened to our request to be taught how to use the looms.

"What?" he said, "You guys, weaving?"

He looked over to Reshat.

"Sure, why not?" we said.

"So you want to learn how to weave?"

"Why so surprised? Weaving's no great skill, is it?"

The two brothers chuckled.

"You know," Reshat said to his elder brother, "they think weaving will be like playing football..."

"So it seems," said Ahmet. "Let's see your hands..."

We held them out.

"Why you poor little things... Look at those soft hands... Now you look at mine."

His were hard and calloused.

"We don't want to carry on living off our parents," explained Gazi, "just tell us: Will you teach us weaving, or not?"

"We don't mind teaching you," said Ahmet, "but..."

"But what?"

"You wouldn't last a week!"

Having promised us they would have words with the foreman, they sent us away from the commercial neighbourhood.

A short time later Hasan Hussein got to hear of all this, and got extremely angry.

"You," he said, pulling me to one side, "shouldn't be going along with him! You should know better than that!"

"I should? What do you mean?"

"I mean don't forget who your father is..."

Gazi, oblivious to the implicit insult, was a little distance away, a cigarette hanging from his mouth, his hands stuck in the pockets of his flared trousers, kicking small stones at an imaginary goal.

II

I got up before dawn the following day, and quietly sneaked out of the house. I slung my jacket across my shoulder, and lit a cigarette. I struck the match like an experienced weaver, and lit the cigarette the way an experienced weaver would. And, with all the arrogance of a weaver who knew his looms, I blew a large mouthful of smoke up towards the sky.

Gazi was waiting for me by his door. He had his jacket slung across his shoulder too.

"How's it going?" I asked.

"Great," he said.

We hadn't noticed that his father had been watching us from the window.

"Huh," he shouted down, "just look at you. See what happens to you without an education!"

As we walked around the corner, Gazi cursed and swore at people who got an education.

"Just give me a cigarette!" he said.

A little while later we got to the main road, feeling keen and hopeful. Women, men, children, workers... A whole sea of people filled the road, and we dived in among them.

We got to the factory and as soon as we entered, my head started spinning at the tumultuous clacking of the looms. It was as if the whole place was galloping towards me. The factory was one large haze of dust, shaking and quaking with its complex pattern of clacking. Cotton particles were everywhere, and I was hit by a smell of starch. Ahmet led me further in by the arm, laughing at my reaction. I felt that the other workers were staring at me incredulously, and finding us as amusing as Ahmet and Reshat obviously were. I remembered feeling this way when I first started at the printing press in Beirut.

Ahmet, in charge of two machines, stood facing me. He couldn't stop chuckling, and looked as if he couldn't believe his eyes. Every now and then he would briefly attend to a broken thread, pull at it in an obviously experienced manner, and expertly tie a knot before turning his attention back to me.

"What are you staring at?" I eventually asked.

"Nothing…" he said.

"No, really, what is it?"

"I was just looking at you, and wondering at God's mysterious ways…"

"Why? What about?"

"Why do you think? That the son of such a great man should be coming to a guy like me…"

I hadn't come across such a deferential attitude at any point in my life.

"I've worked as a waiter in my time, I'll have you know. And I enjoyed it too. Forget about all that. We're all equal in the eyes of God, eh? I'm no soft, spoilt kid!"

In spite of what I was saying, he was still shaking his head, still wondering at the mysterious ways of God.

"This is what we call a shuttle," he said finally, holding up a small, torpedo-like object. The shiny wooden object had pointed ends, and was painted a bright yellow.

"Now this shuttle is empty. When it's empty, you have to open it like this, take out the spindle like this, replace it with a full one like this, close it like this, and throw it from here like… that."

"…?"

"That's the tension arm."

"…?"

"The harnesses. Sley…"

"…?"

I was overwhelmed by the smell of starch, the cloud of cotton dust and the incessant clacking. I had all but forgotten about Istanbul and the rest of our plans. Ahmet interrupted my bout of coughing.

"And this is what it's like at our factory!" he said, "My brother and I have been swallowing this dust since we were this high. Our lungs must be full of the stuff by now!"

Then we went out towards the toilets, and lit up. My ears were ringing. The corridor was covered in graffiti such as 'The House of Lords', 'Dynamo Salih', 'Sit on this', 'Bekir was here' and all sorts of other stuff. Ahead of us was the row of toilets.

"Why do these toilets only have half a door?" I asked.

"That's so that people don't waste time here," explained Ahmet, "and so that the caretaker can easily check the toilets."

"Why would anyone want to spend lots of time on a toilet?"

"You'll see why once you've been around a while. People prefer to waste time on a toilet than to stand around breathing dust. You start thinking of things when you're here... I tell you, once I'm on the toilet and my mind wanders, I could be anywhere in the world. I close my eyes, and I drift away..."

The caretaker was blowing his whistle, and badgering the workers back onto the factory floor. We threw our cigarette butts into the dirty water that went streaming past under the toilets, and returned to the machines.

I don't know how I made it to the end of the day. Gazi seemed to be as tired as I was, and covered in dust.

"How was it?" I asked.

"Not fun..." he said.

I pointed to the crowd of female workers passing by in front of us.

"How about the one in the middle," I asked, "shall we go for it?"

He gave me a disapproving look.

"What's up? Why the dirty look?"

"Here I am, absolutely shattered, and there you go..."

My grandmother was waiting for me by the street door.

"What's this?" she demanded, "Where have you been?"

"School," I lied, "we had a volleyball match..."

"Don't you lie to me, you haven't been to school in a long time. I know you haven't. So, let's have the truth. Where have you been?"

"I said I was at school!"

"So where did all this dust, these bits of cotton come from?"

I gave up.

"I've been working. At a factory."

"What did you just say?"

"A factory!"

"What factory?"

"It's just a normal factory... I'm working on the looms."

She leaned forward.

"Are you really?"

"Honestly!"

"You're doing manual labour?"

"Yes, I'm doing manual labour!"

She gave off such a wail...

I got in and took off my clothes, and had a good wash. She was sitting on the edge of the sofa, her back straight and rigid. I stretched myself out on the divan. After a while, she gently walked over to me.

"You were only teasing, weren't you?"

I didn't reply.

"I knew you were," she went on, "I knew you were teasing. My boy has ambition! He wouldn't stoop to that sort of thing! You know, when you were little, your aunts used to ask you what you wanted to be when you grew up, and you would tell them that you were going to be the most famous doctor in Turkey! As if my boy would do manual labour..."

Inside me, I heard Ahmet's clean, honest laughter, and saw Reshat's fair, boyish looks. I nearly swore at the old woman. She just pottered off, oblivious, mumbling some prayer to herself.

III

The following day and the next, I had to quarrel with my grandmother to get out of the door. Gazi and I would sling our jackets over our shoulders, light our cigarettes, and march off to the factory. We quickly learned the ropes. Ahmet regularly left the machines to me and went off. I was now as good as he was at tying up the loose ends, pulling the threads through, cutting off the roll of cloth, and warping the loom. So was Gazi. And when our day's work was finally over, we'd have time to chat about girls.

"Yep. That's all the training you're getting," said Ahmet one day, "I'll go now and tell the supervisor, but he'll probably want to test you, so be ready!"

He went and told him. The supervisor came along. He was a tall, thin, dark-skinned, shifty looking character, and his eyes were red with trachoma. He asked me to stop my machine. I pulled the disengaging lever and stopped the machine. He snapped off four or five threads, and asked me to pull and tie them. I quickly did so. After getting me to cut off the bolt of woven material, and warp the loom afresh, he seemed satisfied.

"Well done!" he said, "I'll make sure you get the first machine that becomes available."

I then found out that Gazi had passed as well. But when was a machine going to become available? When were we going to start earning, so we could save up and go?

None of the machines looked like becoming available any time soon. And all of the experienced workers had trainees working with them for free. And most of the trainees had quickly learnt their job, passed their tests with flying colours, and they'd all been told that they would get the first machine that became available.

Of course we didn't realise that we were all simply "spares" until much later. The managers of the factory only had us trained up to keep the experienced workers in check. I only found out from a real-life demonstration of their attitude, which ended up with me getting my own machine.

It happened at a machine that was two machines over from where we were.

Then one day, the machine operated by Kurd Dursun suddenly threw a shuttle, and Albanian Nuri collapsed. We all ran over. His mouth was opening and closing like a fish. It seems that the shuttle had got him in the ear. Someone went and told the factory floor supervisor. The supervisor came, inspected the wounded man, and went off in a hurry. He quickly returned with the short, fat chief machinist, the heavyweight administrator, the stubby-nosed managing director and the owner himself, who scuttled along at an angle, carrying his huge midriff on a skinny pair of legs and outsized feet. Everyone started speaking at once, and they all started barking out instructions. Meanwhile, our foreman went over to the mains switch and pulled it down. The whole factory came to a halt.

Kurd Dursun, whose machine had thrown the shuttle, looked as white as a sheet. The owner of the factory started shouting and swearing. At one point looked as if he was about to slap someone, but Kurd Dursun grabbed hold of his raised arm and pushed him away. That caused uproar. Someone went for someone else, people jeered and whistled, it was complete pandemonium. I looked over and saw Dursun's boots, moving around at head height. The crowd had grabbed hold of him, lifted him up, and were unceremoniously bundling him out of the factory.

Ahmet, right next to me, swore loudly for all to hear. He then pulled me aside.

"Come on. We're off to have a cigarette."

We got to the toilets' corridor.

"Well!" I said, "What do you think will happen now?"

Ahmet was nervously tapping the ash off his cigarette, as if preoccupied with something else.

"What'll happen about what?" he asked. "You saw it: The machine threw a shuttle. Got the man right in the ear. So now they're trying to blame poor Dursun, so that if the man dies or something they won't have to pay compensation. But really..."

He spat hard at the concrete floor through his teeth.

"Half the fault's with the machines, but the other half's with our supervisor..."

"Why's that?"

"The supplier's a relative of his. All the warp we get has knots in it. When the shuttle hits a knot, whap! Off it goes. Oh, he knows this happens, but he won't do anything about it."

"Might Albanian Nuri die, then?"

"He could..."

"He could actually die, really?"

"I remember another time when a shuttle came flying off a machine, just like this. It hit a good mate, 'Laz' Haydar. Bless him, he was a lovely guy, and a man true to his word. I mean, if you said Haydar, mate, let's do such and such, he'd be right in there, come hell or high water. Anyway this shuttle flew off, smacked him right in the ear, and caused internal bleeding. Poor guy dropped dead on the spot. You know, I've lost my mother, I've lost my father, but I never cried as much as I did when poor Haydar died. And you know why? Because he was a true friend; Always there for you!

"He died, huh?"

"Dropped dead on the spot. That's what death's like here. Gets you before you know it..."

"Is Albanian Nuri married?"

"With four children. His wife's a strong woman, though. He took her from the thread-making section here, in this factory. She's from Crete, but she's a true Ottoman."

"They'll pay compensation to his children if he dies, won't they?"

"That would depend on our statements. Didn't you see what happened? The whole lot of them turned against poor Dursun. And you know why? It's so they can make it out to be his negligence. If he's the one who's found negligent under the Law, and they say that that caused the accident..."

"Dursun's going to get dropped in it!"

"That's what'll happen..."

We returned to the factory floor. The owner, our supervisor, the administrator, the chief machinist and everyone else was there. They had gathered the workers around. They all seemed to be arguing. We moved in among them. We couldn't make out precisely what was going on, but there was clearly some sort of disagreement with lots of people raising their voices. Then one of the weavers, whom I recognised from his black glasses, pushed his way through the crowd towards the centre. I could tell from his tone of voice that he was being calm and collected. But people behind him started pushing and shoving.

"We're not!" yelled someone. Shouts of, "We're not! No, we're not!" started echoing among the crowd, there was a sudden confusion, people jumped at each other, and Ahmet bolted forward. Shuttles started flying through the air, and I heard swearing. People were chasing each other among the machines. One large shuttle whistled past my head, and another smashed into one of the light-bulbs. I saw a pair of black glasses fly into the air...

All this carried on for some time. Then, police appeared at the factory doors. Seven, eight, maybe ten or more of them. They blew their whistles as they came in, much of the woven cloth got torn, but eventually things calmed down. Police carted off many of the weavers, most of them with bleeding lips and torn clothes. Ahmet had acquired a nasty gash on one eyebrow, and his eye had swollen. He was shaking. He suddenly darted forward again. He went up to the police chief, said a few things in an angry tone, and came back.

"You keep an eye on the machines," he said to me, "I'll be back shortly."

"Where are you going?"

"They're taking some of the lads away, and I can't leave them on their own. I'll get them to take my statement, and then I'll be right back."

He picked up his jacket from the metal bar where it had been hanging, and left.

When the day was over, I finally got to see Gazi.

"How about that?" he said. "Do you think we'll get to work after all this?"

"I have no idea..."

"What do you think of these flying shuttles?"

"Ahmet says that any of us could die at any time. He says you could be dead before you know it!"

"I thought all hell was breaking loose. These factory workers are really stressed out! Between you and me, I was really worried... And what if we get a shuttle in the head one of these days?"

"What do you mean? What are you saying?"

"I'm saying there's a danger of getting a shuttle in the head... Got a cigarette?"

"Yeah, I've got a cigarette. You think you might get a shuttle in the head – what if you do?"

"Think about it! Give me those matches... What do you think would happen? How would you feel, pushing up the daisies?"

"Well, it wouldn't really be the end of the world if the great Gazi was gone, now, would it?"

"Who says it wouldn't be? What would you do without me?"

On our way back, we met our team captain. He was cycling along on his crooked bicycle. He saw us and stopped. He harshly demanded to know why we hadn't been to training recently. So we told him. He thought we should be ashamed of ourselves. How could anyone with any self-respect go and spend all day on a loom?

"Listen lads, the league games are coming up soon, and you must come to all the training sessions. OK?"

Gazi and I looked at each other.

"What are you looking at each other for?" asked the captain, "We'll see you alright at the club... So, is that understood? I want you at the training sessions, giving your all..."

And off he went on his crooked bicycle, becoming little more than a large bottom in golf trousers, disappearing into the distance.

"He said that they'd see us alright at the club," said Gazi, "you heard him!"

"So? A fiver a week, or a tenner, tops. Then what?"

"I know it won't be much, but you've got to think of this shuttle thing..."

"Meaning...?"

"Meaning, it's just not worth..." he started, and then he laughed.

"That's all well and good," I said, "but we'd be letting down Ahmet and Reshat if we left."

"Leave it out! What, you'd rather die?"

The next day, we told Ahmet of our decision.

"I knew it!" he said, "I said you were soft! You want easy money, don't you? A desk job somewhere, a nice little pen and a bit of paper..."

We didn't leave immediately. You see, they sacked a whole bunch of the workers, and filled all their vacancies with us, their "spares". So, at the end of it all, we did get to work our own machines, but at what cost?

We quit.

IV

The league games had started, and so had the athletics competitions. As there was a huge shortfall between the food we ate and the calories we burned, both Gazi and I lost a lot of weight. We became ashamed of our skinny legs and washboard chests.

That evening I went to bed having only eaten a quarter-loaf of bread, sprinkled with a mixture of salt, red pepper and cinnamon. That's all my grandmother could manage, now that it was nearing the end of the month.

We had athletics competitions the following afternoon. I was to run the two-hundred, the fifteen-hundred, and the four by one-hundred relay.

"Remember lads," the team captain said, "you're not to eat meat at lunch! And definitely no onions!"

He was apparently saying that because we couldn't run our best if we'd eaten those!

We played table-tennis at the clubhouse, and chatted. Gazi teased Hasan Hussein, and we talked about the races that afternoon. But although we were talking about the races, I couldn't help but notice that Hasan Hussein was chain-smoking!

Now there were forty of us, and we all knew each other very well. So I went over and stood by his side... And saw that the tips of cigarettes were even decorated with shiny foil! I mean, us and fancy cigarettes?

"Where did you get those from?" I asked.

"Don't ask. I've set aside your share, so don't worry. But don't tell Gazi!"

"Well, OK... But where did they come from?"

"I said don't ask! Heavens' sake!"

But I had to know. I carried on pestering him. How could I not know? Maybe he'd found some buried treasure or something... I cornered him in a quiet spot. He was sniggering to himself. He reached into the back pocket of his baggy trousers, and pulled out a blue packet.

"Look at all these fags! And you've got your share set aside! But please don't tell Gazi, he'd only go and spoil it all..."

"I want to know where they all came from!"

"Bloody hell! You don't let up, do you? Look the deal is, you get your share – but no questions asked. Right?"

"Come on... You know I can keep a secret..."

"I'm not so sure... I want you to swear you won't tell anyone!"

I did.

"The captain," he explained, "had forgotten them on the table."

"So you..."

"So I... Well, you know... Look, I asked him for one, and he said no. Said I'd get out of breath and wouldn't be able to run properly this afternoon."

"What if he notices?"

"No chance... How could he? It's not as if he's short of supplies!"

Just as he said that, the captain came running in. Hasan Hussein blanched. But there was nothing to worry about. He had brought in our studded shoes, and started to hand them out. Then he pulled a fiver out of his wallet.

"Could you do me favour," he asked Hasan Hussein, "and go and get me a packet of Bosphorus cigarettes?"

Hasan Hussein's colour returned to normal. He grabbed the money, and shot off.

Our captain was a complete sports fanatic. He'd race around the clubhouse all day like a speeding machine, go in and out of all the rooms, and attend to each and every member of the team. He'd be with you one minute, with someone else the next. He was like that now, explaining for the umpteenth time how to start a race, and what would constitute a false start. As Hasan Hussein handed him his cigarettes, he was explaining the things we had to pay particular attention to when exchanging batons in the four by one hundred.

I hadn't eaten lunch. There'd been nothing for me to eat. Well, one slice of bread, but that had been it. One slice of plain, dry bread.

In the two hundred, I came second by a fraction of a second.

We won the four by one hundred. But my heart was pounding too hard, and my vision was going dark... My stomach was rumbling, and I felt quite sick. Then, they called me up for the fifteen hundred. I knew that the earth wasn't swaying really, and that the trees weren't changing position.

"This is it!" said the captain, "This is it now! We have to win this race. If we do – and there's no reason why we shouldn't – overall we'll be ahead on points. Just grit your teeth, and do it…"

I broke out in a cold sweat.

"You didn't eat meat this lunchtime, did you?"

"I beg you pardon? Did you say meat? Who, me?"

"Yes, you…"

"No, no I didn't."

"Good. Save up your appetite; you can eat whatever you want tonight!"

"…???"

My legs were shaky, and my eyebrow was twitching. I think there were seven of us, all lined up at the start. We heard the sudden crack of the starter pistol, and off we went. The first lap went by, and we were on to the second… My vision grew darker, and my stomach felt worse. It felt as if the earth was sliding around under my studded boots. What was going on?

Lap three. I was running past the captain, and I was really pushing myself to go on. The others were only a couple of steps behind me. The captain had a cigarette dangling from his lips, and his pale face seemed even paler than usual.

"Open up," he yelled, "pull away!"

A final effort, and I pulled away a bit more.

We were on the fourth lap now. Around the middle of the lap. I'm still ahead… I was approaching the end of the fourth lap when suddenly, I felt as if I'd been hit over the head with a tree-trunk, and the world went topsy-turvy.

When I opened my eyes, I saw a bright moon shining in a navy sky… Gazi was by my side.

"What happened?" I asked.

"Stay still!" he said.

"OK, but why?"

"Shut up, and just stay still!"

"Did I pass out?"

"Yes, you passed out and ruined it for everybody!"

I slowly sat up. It was night-time, and the cool air of night made the silvery light of the moon seem cold. My whole body felt stiff. Then I suddenly remembered everything, and felt my hunger return with a vengeance.

"You'd better stay out of the captain's way!"

"Why?"

"You lost the fifteen hundred, so we ended up in second place on points, thanks to you!"

Hasan Hussein intervened.

"You idiot!" he said, "What did you have to go and faint for?"

He was presumably joking. They both held me on either side, handed me my rolled up clothes, and got me into a cab. Hasan Hussein gave the driver a doctor's address.

"Why there?" I asked.

"You're ill, aren't you?"

"Who, me?"

"Yes, you..."

"I'm not ill or anything! Forget about the doctor's.

"Why did you faint then?"

I leant over, and whispered in his ear. He burst out laughing.

"Well then! Hey, cabbie! Take us to Silo's Kebabs!"

We entered the crowded restaurant to a tantalising smell of meat. Hasan Hussein turned to one of the waiters with all the airs of a rich man.

"Excuse me! Attend to the gentlemen, please!"

What? Is this the same Hasan Hussein we knew?

"Hasan, mate," said Gazi, "are you sure about this? I mean, I'm totally broke, and so is he..."

Hasan Hussein was deadly serious.

"Excuse me, waiter! Attend to the gentlemen!"

We ordered our kebabs. This had really perked us up... But how were we going to pay for it?

Hasan Hussein offered us fancy cigarettes from his blue packet, which we then stuck behind our ears as the kebabs arrived, and all three of us dived into our food in a frenzy.

After we had eaten, while we were washing our hands, Hasan Hussein whispered in my ear and explained where the money had come from.

"You know when I brought back the captain's cigarettes? Well I had all his change, and there was all the commotion…"

V

My grandmother wrote to my youngest aunt begging her to take me in, telling her about my weaving job and how the way I was carrying on was very worrying. My youngest aunt lived in an Istanbul suburb, and was married to a gentleman in commerce. She acted immediately.

We received a letter from her; it was fifteen pages long. The letter was addressed to me.

"… You can't do whatever you feel like! What will people say? As soon as you receive the money I'm sending, you're to come immediately…"

I told Gazi first. His eyes lit up.

"Oh, wow, would you believe it? That's brilliant!"

"Yes," I said, "but you'll end up staying here…"

"Forget us lot. I'll come along with you though, if you want. I'm fed up of my mother nagging me anyway. Off we'll go, we'll get ourselves jobs, or we'll get into Gedikli. That'll be easiest."

"And when we graduate from Gedikli, we can marry our girlfriends!"

"Forget about the girlfriends. Your aunt's money is enough to get us both there. We'll go by boat, travelling on the open deck."

Our decision made, we thought of Hasan Hussein. We decided to keep this from him. There would be no problem telling the girls, though. After all, they did love us, and lived for us...

That night we went back to the old sycamore, and signalled the girls to come out with our matches. They came. We told them. My one started to cry.

"You're lying!" she said, "You'll forget all about us as soon as you get there!"

How could we? We lived for them too. What value would our lives have, if not for them?

Three days later, clutching my old suitcase I'd brought with me from Beirut, my threadbare bedding, and my basket, I left my grandmother's.

When I got to the train station the girls were there and, in spite of everything, so was Hasan Hussein. My girl had her head on her sister's shoulder and was crying. Hasan Hussein had again removed his glass eye, and was wiping it with his handkerchief. Then the third bell went, the engine blew its whistle, and the train started to move. Handkerchiefs were waving, and my girl still had her head on her sister's shoulder.

Gazi was to board the train at the next station. When the train got there he leapt on: Empty hands, empty pockets, and half a packet of cigarettes. It was his first proper journey anywhere. He was chain-smoking, spitting and, although he had no such habit, biting his nails.

"My left ear's humming!" he complained at one point.

"What if my father hears of me running away?" he asked a little later.

"What if he does?" I asked, "So what?"

"Could he have me sent back?"

"No he couldn't!" I said, "You're over eighteen, your father can't have you sent back from anywhere. Don't worry, the Law's on our side!"

He paused.

"My poor father," he murmured, "he was saying how his vision sometimes darkened, how sometimes he felt dizzy. And he has kidney stones..."

He sighed deeply, and flicked away his cigarette butt.

When we arrived at Mersin, we bought two of the cheapest tickets and went down to the port. There, some way away over the flickering sea, the ship that was to take us away was busily releasing clouds of black smoke into the evening sky. We were taken to it on a small boat. Once on board, we placed my things in a corner of the hold, and went up on deck. We looked back at the twinkling light of the brightly lit city of Mersin.

"My poor father!" repeated Gazi, "What with his kidney stones and all..."

He rested his head against the iron railings.

The sadness of the evening, Gazi, the shimmering lights of the city, the sea... I felt like crying. The slowly darkening sea somehow made me think of death. I felt sad inside, and remembered my little sister who died years ago, when she was only four. I thought of her tiny little coffin, the narrow little grave, and her dainty little gravestone. I felt as if we may be lost in these waters forever.

"How much money do we have left?" asked Gazi, suddenly.

"We have seventy-five kurus." I said.

"I've no cigarettes left either."

So I went and bought him a cheap seven-and-a-half kurus packet. Then we went down to the hold, over to our stuff. We spread out my bedding, and sat down next to each other. Over to one side of the hold, an elderly man had turned his cap back to front, and was engaged in his evening prayers. Over on the other, a young man with a red waistband was drinking raki. There were women in purdah, naughty boys running around, and young girls who had to stay kneeling on the floor demurely for hours on end... We only paid attention to one family in that entire crowd, though. Well, I say family, and we did know the couple from Adana, but... The woman was quite old and wrinkled, and had too much make-up on, and we knew that the one-armed man she referred to as her "husband" was a pimp. But who cares? We re-introduced ourselves, and we were soon on familiar terms.

The woman had a beautiful, graceful daughter. The raucous laughter of the mother revealed nicotine stained teeth, and the daughter was clearly embarrassed by this.

"Mother!" she would say, every so often.

The woman didn't care at all. She laughed, chatted, made eyes, kept touching us, lit one cigarette after another, and generally talked non-stop. Within half an hour, we had her full life story. Well, the sort of story that one always expects from a woman like this: They inevitably come from a noble family, but then their husband cheats on them, so their womanly pride gets injured, and then for the sake of their honour...

But she was marvellously open-handed. Every time she lit a cigarette she thought of us, and if we tried to decline insisted with a "Go on, go on..." Even though I wasn't much of a smoker, I thought of what Gazi would be like later, so I accepted the cigarettes, took two puff off each, then put them out and pocketed them.

As I stared at the woman's – Zumrut's – blackened teeth, I must have drifted off to sleep. When I woke up, it was morning. A breakfast feast had been spread out and Gazi, who clearly hadn't even given his face a wash, was already sitting cross-legged by the food.

"Come on," he said, when he saw I was awake. "We're going to have breakfast. We were just waiting for you to wake up."

I took one long look at him. Then I left, saying I was going to wash my hands and face. I did not go back. Out on the deck, the morning breeze was cool, and the sea was calm. Our ship was moving along, quite close to the shore.

A flustered Gazi appeared by my side.

"Why didn't you come and have breakfast?"

I just looked at him. He laughed.

"Leave it out. This is no time for pride. What do you think of the daughter, though, eh?"

"Hmm?"

"The girl. Quite something, isn't she?"

"Shame on you!"

"Why?"

"What about her back home?"

He wandered off, whistling.

I stayed on deck until the sun was high in the sky, watching the dolphins. They were chasing the ship, stubbornly tailing us. The wrinkled skin of the sea, now a dull green under the bright sun, reflected the sunlight back, as if it were a mirror smashed into millions of tiny pieces.

I went down into the hold. Zumrut was still talking. Gazi was by her daughter's knees, already friends with her. Knowing that any comment under such circumstances is bound to fall on deaf ears, I ignored them. Gazi was happy with that. The others were as well. In fact, I was happy for things to be this way. At least I didn't have the mouth and the cigarettes to put up with.

I went up on deck again.

The next day passed in much the same way.

As soon as Gazi mentioned he was getting hungry, the mother and the daughter immediately spread out the sheet to put food down for him. If anything, the mother was keener. And Gazi wasn't waiting to be asked, he was just tucking in.

As for the one armed man the woman referred to as "my husband"...

He was really quiet. He would escort Zumrut to the toilets now and again, and help put the food out and clear up afterwards, but otherwise he just sat there, listening to Zumrut all day.

We didn't mix much with any of the other passengers. Most of them were there for short distances, and got off soon after they boarded. Peasants, tradesmen...

At one of the small ports we stopped at on our third night, a young man boarded the ship. He was dark, athletic, good looking, and played the harmonica beautifully. He did the Charleston as well as Caucasian and West-Anatolian folk dances. The atmosphere in the hold was transformed by his arrival. He too, like us, was off to Istanbul in search of his destiny. He'd wangled himself a ticket somehow, left his girlfriend behind, and was off to seek his fortune...

"If I manage to get into Gedikli," he – Hasan – told us, "it'll be good. If not, I have this friend in Galata, called Nevzat... He works shovelling coal. I'll just have to go and live off him. He'll make sure I'm alright."

"Did you say Gedikli? That's where we're headed..."

"You too? Really? Well, I'm hoping that this time..."

"This time?"

"Five years... For five years now, I've been going there year after year, trying to get in, but getting nowhere."

"...?"

"I live with my poor old mother... I don't remember my dad. Apparently, he was a fisherman. Lads around our way don't usually remember their dads..."

"Why not?"

"They go fishing throughout the year. So when they leave one morning, and don't come back that night, no-one's really that surprised. The mothers around our way have to be our fathers too!"

Zumrut and her daughter disembarked that day, at a picturesque little port set among orange groves. Gazi was leaning on the iron railings, looking at where they'd gone, even tough they had disappeared long since.

I nudged his shoulder.

"And now?"

He sighed.

"Give me a cigarette!"

I took out one of the cigarettes I had put out quickly and kept especially for him.

"What do you call that?"

I explained. He burst out laughing.

"Well done, mate!" he said, "We're ready for anything now!"

"And that girl?"

"Oh, forget about her."

"Really? Why?"

"It wasn't the girl I was after anyway; it was her mother's cigarettes, and the food. That's all that was."

"Don't worry about being broke," said Hasan, "or about going hungry or anything. If things get a bit tight we can always shovel some coal into the furnace in the boiler room. But it won't come to that: We can help traders with their loading and unloading."

He was right: We didn't end up having to shovel coal. We helped the traders load and unload all along the route. We weren't earning much but, on the other hand, we weren't starving either. Then one day, the ninth day of our voyage, we woke to the long, croaky sound of the ship's horn.

"We're there!" said Hasan.

We rushed up on deck. The ship was anchoring at Galata.

Istanbul was shrouded in a fine mist. We were facing the Galata Bridge. Trams were shuttling to and fro, and people were milling around, looking like a mass of ants from this distance. The dirty waters of the port were crowded with barges and steamers. The hubbub of voices permeated the blanket of smoke and the smell of coal.

"Well I never," marvelled Gazi, "Well I never…"

"What's that?"

"Well, I mean, it's Istanbul, Istanbul itself! Look at that beauty!"

Hasan took us over to his friend's, the coal worker Nevzat's place in Galata. Hooked nosed Nevzat was black all over, and had his sleeves rolled up to his elbows. He smiled, baring two shiny white rows of teeth.

"As you have nowhere else to stay," he said, "you're more than welcome to stay here."

Then he offered us some bread with some white cheese and a few boiled eggs.

"You'll have to excuse me," he said, "but I have to get to work. My room is yours."

It was a tiny, narrow room. The floor was littered with onion skins and empty raki bottles, and there was a pile of filthy pots to one side...

"What do you think of my friend, then?" asked Hasan, "Just like I told you, eh?"

He pointed out a picture of a pretty woman, stuck up on the wall with four drawing pins.

"He used to live with this woman," he explained, "until he caught this dreadful disease off her. Anyone else would have murdered the bitch. But not him. On the contrary, he paid to have her treated, and then sent her on her way. Never saw her again. He's a good lad, is our Nevzat. Sound."

There's so much in Istanbul to amaze people like us, fresh in from the sticks.

It's marvellous!

For all its wonders, though, what use does Istanbul have for a young man who has just stepped off a boat with all of sixty kurus to his name?

So, the three of us set off to Karakoy, went up Bankalar road, and over to Pera. Gazi was wide-eyed every step of the way. He was completely lost for words.

That day we toured Istanbul, that wonderful city of legends. We were so mesmerised by it all, we completely forgot about our girlfriends and the Gedikli Academy. We were ready to die for any one of the stunning women we were seeing...

VI

Eventually we had our fill of the wonders of Istanbul. This was because we were almost always feeling hungry, and beautiful sights didn't fill our stomachs. It was high time we found ourselves some work.

Yes, work!

But where?

We were free men, as far as that goes. We were free to set up a factory, or walk into any restaurant in Istanbul and order whatever we wanted. But we didn't want to set up a factory or walk into, say, Tokatliyan's, and order food. I guess we just didn't know how to make the most of this freedom.

One day, when we were wandering aimlessly, once again in the grip of hunger pangs, who should we come across in Aksaray but old Cemal! You remember – who bought himself a cold drink with our stamp money instead of posting our letter?

After hugging and jumping all over each other so much that passers-by were starting to stare, we started to catch up.

He had got into Gedikli last year. So we asked if we might be able to get in. He shook his head sadly. There were so many applicants... Having said that, our chance was as good as anyone else's, so why not?

"But hang on guys," he said, "you remember Memet, you know, the twenty-six year-old?"

"Our captain?"

"Yeah, him. He's here, over in Beykoz. He works in a night-club that has a restaurant. It's a cushy number. If you're here to work, his boss could probably get you jobs at the Beykoz shoe factory. All the foremen and people from the factory eat there.

"That's all for later, mate," said Gazi, "This idiot's too stuck up to say anything, but we've not had a thing to eat since yesterday. We can't think straight anymore. Come on mate, how much have you got on you?"

Cemal cheked his pockets.

"Not much, I'm afraid. I could get you guys some bread and cheese..."

"And a packet of cigarettes. I've had it with left-over butts!"

"As we're going for it," I added, "a cup of coffee would go down a treat."

"Leave it out, guys! Forget about cigarettes and coffee, right?"

"Believe me Cemal, mate, we can't simply forget about cigarettes or coffee."

The next day we latched onto Cemal, and off we went to Beykoz!

When we got there, Cemal led us to a tiny little restaurant, nestling among whispering trees by the side of the road.

"The food here is amazing," he confided, "let's just sit ourselves down...

"So, the food here is amazing..." Gazi whispered to me, "Look, you'd better not stop me from eating my fill again. I'll eat as many portions as I can!"

"What are you like? You'll totally put them off from doing us any favours!"

"Why should I put them off? I'm fed up with your attitude! Just don't interfere. I'm going to get stuck in."

We pulled up a chair each. Cemal returned with Memet. And there he was; the captain of our neighbourhood football team. When he saw us he was stunned at first, and then delighted. Then, he lost his good humour. He thought that we had come over to watch the legendary Fenerbahce play football, and to spend money. But we were only talking about getting some work. Well, yes, he explained, of course we were friends, but he didn't own the restaurant. He made enough to eat, but that was it. And the boss was an awkward man. No, he didn't think he'd let us eat on credit. Working at the Beykoz shoe factory? We really came out with these impossible ideas, didn't we? We should see what it was like outside the gates there. There were queues of people dying for work, and not people like us, skilled cobblers who'd once had their own businesses!

I looked at Gazi, and he looked at me. Gazi's fists were

resting on his waist, shaking. Cemal was bitterly regretting bringing us all the way here.

"Come on," he pleaded, "at least put the guys up for a couple of days!"

"To be honest with you Cemal," said Memet, "I don't know if I can. If the restaurant was mine, there'd be no question, obviously. But I only work here... As for the boss, well, he's meant to be my friend from the Balmumcu orphanage, but you have no idea what he's like."

Gazi, now on the verge of tears, grabbed me by the arm.

"Come on, we're going!"

He indicated the hills in the distance.

"Well head out that way!"

"Shame on you!" said Cemal, "Call yourself a friend? Call yourself a human being? You were starving when we found you in Adana. If it wasn't for us... Forgotten all that now, have you?"

"Oh Cemal, of course I haven't forgotten, I know... God bless you all, how could I forget? You all helped me out so much, but..."

"There are no ifs or buts about it. Go and talk to your boss. Now!"

Memet gulped, and turned towards the back of the restaurant, looking around.

"Alright," said Gazi, "Where is he? I'll talk to him."

Memet gestured towards one of the crowded tables.

"He's the one standing there his back to us. With the white shirt, holding the tray."

Gazi strode forward, and Cemal and I followed.

Gazi took the man to one side.

"Look sir," he explained, "We're friends of that useless waiter of yours. We've come all the way from Adana. We've no work, no money, and to be frank, we're starving. Could you possibly put us up for a couple of days?"

The man looked us up and down.

"Had you come all the way here thinking that he owned the place?"

Gazi told him the full story. The man laughed out loud.

"So, you lads heard that Istanbul's streets were paved with gold?"

He called Memet. Memet ran to his side.

"Look," said his boss, "they came here thinking you owned the place. They heard the streets of Istanbul were paved with gold. Why are you sending them away?"

Memet blushed.

"Come on now," said his boss, "get them some chairs to sit on, offer them a drink. Now that we're running this charity, we might as well look after them! Oh, and feed the poor beggars!"

We took the chairs, feeling small and embarrassed. We carried them out behind the cafeteria, onto the grass. We sat down, and lit up.

"Don't let it bug you," said Memet, "he always talks that way. You should hear what he calls me!"

We pretended not to care. We sat there an hour, then two, then until it was dark. We talked about Yorgi, about Ahmet the coffee shop owner, about Mendiye, about our football games, how if 'Meatball' Ahmet had played in the final against Kubilayspor instead of 'Croupier' Bayram we might have won, how if only the free kick had been taken by Gazi, and not 'Dodge' Ali, then it would have been a dead cert, and how grocer Nuri kept going on about the membership fees he kept paying even though he never got to play a single game…

Gazi slapped Cemal playfully on his cap.

"You useless oaf! Remember the day you nicked our stamp money to get a cold drink?"

"Yeah… Those were the days. Mind you, I was dying of thirst!"

"We had to walk all bloody night because of you!"

"Yorgi sold his wristwatch then, do you remember? Good old Yorgi."

"He was better when he had the bran shop... Now he's really rich, in the drapery business."

"Really?" said Memet, "So he finally married his uncle's daughter? And what about Saim?"

"He's graduating from high school this year, and wants to get into Law. Says he's going to be a judge."

"And 'Dodge' Ali? Salih? Hunchback Rejep?"

"You don't want to know about hunchback Rejep..."

"Why? What happened?"

"He died."

"No, really?"

"Yeah, it was awful, the poor sod... His body was crawling with worms when they found him."

It was getting dark, and we sat silently, listening to the rustling of the leaves, and the distant hoots of ships traversing the Bosphorus.

"And what about old Hasan Hussein?" asked Memet, "Is he an accountant yet?"

"No, but he will be."

"He will be, huh?"

"He will."

Memet sniggered.

"What's so funny?"

"I just remembered the day he stuffed his pockets full of fruit compote..."

"And then there was that time with our captain's cigarettes..."

"And that day he ordered us kebabs?"

"Those were the days alright," mused Gazi, "stuffing our faces one day, starving the next..."

Cemal caught the last ferry back.

"Right then," I said, "Are you really telling me that a city this size, this huge place can't fit in a couple more people like us?"

Memet sighed.

"I hate this poverty! Look, I'm not a bad guy... Come on guys, you know I'm not bad at heart. Not at all, really.

But what can I do? A couple of my friends have come all this way, and really I should be able to go and take them out somewhere, put them up, show them the sights... I mean, I know I should, but I'm tied down here. I don't have that choice..."

I caught Gazi's expression out of the corner of my eye. I could hear people going by on the road behind me, and the sparkling laughter of children chasing each other under the trees.

Memet's boss had come right up to us, and we hadn't heard him.

"So," he said, "you're going to each get a job in Istanbul, earn some money, and send for your girlfriends? You'll be needing a decent place to stay... Plus, most important of all, you'll need a good strong safe each. That's a must. To keep all your saved money in, hmm?"

Fists resting on his waist, he laughed at us.

"If," he continued, "you ever need a cook and a scullion, do let us know. Memet and I are always on the lookout for something better!"

He was laughing as he spoke. He started to walk away, and stopped.

"The restaurant has an attic," he added, "it's not what you might call a guest room, but you'll be OK if you lay down a mat. The weather's warm, so you won't need any covers. The only thing is, there'll be plenty of rats and cockroaches. They might get a bit cheeky, so I'd plug my ears, if I were you. Oh, and I think there's a cracked mirror there, too. You can brush the dust off that and use it. I think it used to belong to some Armenian Nobleman. Used it for his morning ablutions. The only thing is, it doesn't reflect very well. It's a bit warped, and the silver is coming off. Still, it did belong to a nobleman, and even if it isn't worth any money, that's got to count for something, eh? What do you think?"

We didn't reply. He went off, laughing to himself.

Then he called Memet over, and had words with him.

Gazi, meanwhile, was cursing his poverty and at having to put up with this.

VII

The next morning Memet came up to us.

"I'm going into Istanbul," he said, "I'll go to Nevzat's in Galata, and bring your stuff over. Why don't you write out a note I can give him?"

I wrote a brief message, and gave it to Memet.

When he got back, he was looking very pleased with himself. Suspiciously pleased.

"I got there," he explained, "I found Nevzat, and gave him your note. He read it, and he said 'Tell them not to worry about their stuff, it can stay here, I'll look after it. They can pick it up whenever they come back.'"

Memet laid on an excellent feast for us that evening, complete with dolma, salad and raki, and quickly got drunk. He started crying.

"Now take me," he said, "I'm not a bad guy really, you know I'm not, but this poverty, you know…"

He was putting his arms around me, then turning to Gazi and giving him a hug, then back to me.

We ate, we drank, we sat in the park by the sea and watched the sailing ships, shared all our knowledge of stars, made lewd comments about immodest women, and finally went to bed in the early hours. When we woke up, the sun was reflecting off our dusty piece of mirror.

"What did you think of the state Memet was in last night?" asked Gazi.

"I don't know," I said, "It reminds me of Hasan Hussein ordering us those kebabs. If Memet hasn't stumbled on some treasure something must have happened – I'm sure we'll find out sooner or later."

And sure enough, we did.

It was another day at the restaurant, and we felt we had no chance of finding work. The day went by, and late that night, Memet was with his boss, stuffing dolma. The smell of dolma spread through the whole place. We had not had a single bite to eat all day. We were breathing in the smell of the fresh stuffing, and staring straight down at the aubergine dolma, which were lined up on white oval serving plates immediately below us.

"I could eat twenty of those dolma," declared Gazi.

"Don't go getting ideas!"

"No, I'm serious."

We stared at the plates without blinking.

"Later on, we could creep down quietly…" he said.

"And then what?"

"We'd gently lift the glass on the display unit…"

"And?"

"Just take one each…"

"Would you really do that?"

"I don't know. You?"

"Me? I don't think so…"

Gazi swore at Istanbul.

"What a place!" he said, "If my mother was still alive to see me now. Here I am, agonising over a couple of dolma!"

"What about me?" I pointed out, "I never forget once, my brother Niyazi had turned his nose up at the lamb chops at a meal. So my father forced him to eat a couple, and he ran off heaving! We used to have meat delivered by the carcass. Butter was delivered in large bags, and cheese in large cans…"

"And that idiot is taking the mickey out of us."

"Who?"

"Memet's boss."

"Oh what, that stuff the other day? If we ever needed a cook, and all that…"

"And that about what we'd earn and needing a safe. He's taking the mickey. Hey look, I reckon all that dolma stuffing is going to be a bit too much, what do you think?"

"It looks that way. But that's not for us to say, is it?"

"No, but if they have too much stuffing... I mean, if it was all eaten, at least none would be wasted..."

When they had finished, there really was leftover stuffing. But Memet and his bossed got a spoon each, and started tucking in.

I bit down on my lips. Gazi swore, and let out a cough. They looked up, but we pulled back just in time.

"Those idiots asleep?" asked the man.

Memet nodded.

"Are we idiots?" whispered Gazi.

"I don't know; I don't think so..." I whispered back.

"You tell that friend Cemal of yours," said the man, "not to be gathering up all these useless strays and dumping them here. And tell those bums to pack up tomorrow and bugger off!"

Memet hung his head.

"I realise," said the man, "Istanbul's a big city. It's not easy to be broke, to have to wander the streets with no money. It's hard, really hard. I do realise that, but you know the situation we're in... I'd asked you to see Bohor today, did you?"

"To settle his tab? Yes, I saw him. He apologised, and said he'd definitely settle in a couple of days or so."

"Typical! Whoever we go to, it's either payment in a couple of days, or at the end of the month. We owe over a grand ourselves. I don't know how we're going to get through this one. Go and tell those bums that they have to be out tomorrow. I'm not a charity... Let God feed the mouths he created!"

This was followed by a long silence.

Gazi looked at me with his sunken eyes and we just sat there, looking at each other.

The next day Memet didn't have to say anything. We politely asked him for fares back into town. He pretended to be disappointed that we were leaving already.

"Don't think bad of me," he said, "I'm not a bad guy. At the end of the day, I'm only..."

His boss had come over, curious.

"What's up?" he asked, "Off already? You should have stayed until you found some work. What're you going to do, have you decided?"

We told him that we had made no decisions. Gazi and I exchanged glances. Then, having got enough money for the boat fares, we went down to the port.

Then we went back into Istanbul, over to Galata, and found Nevzat. There he was, beaky nose and pearly teeth. It was than that we found out the truth of the matter.

"Short man, beady little eyes, clean shaven. Came here, gave me your note, so I gave all your stuff to him. Then off he went!"

Gazi was livid, and swore and cursed. I simply froze in horror. Nevzat took a long hard look at us, and wandered over to the window, whistling softly to himself. Then he picked up a large tomato that was on the table.

"So…" he continued, "He didn't bring you your stuff?"

"No…"

"What are you going to do now? You've no bedding, no clothes…"

"I don't know."

He looked us up and down again.

"Well, now! That brings me to the second part of my tale. I got your note but, I'm not going to lie to you, I didn't like the look of the man… So I did give him your stuff, but I went and followed him when he left here. Out he went, and so did I. Anyway, to cut a long story short, he took your stuff to this Jewish place down the road, left them there, and off he went. So I went straight in there, walked up to the Jew, and told him that the stuff had just been stolen, and that the police would be over any minute. The Jew had a fit! Anyway, your mate had pawned them for a ten lira note, so I gave the Jew the money, and got your stuff back. It's all downstairs, sitting there. You can pick it up whenever you want!"

Gazi and I went wild! We put our arms around

Nevzat's neck, and hugged him and kissed him...

"As you lads still haven't got jobs," he said, "you can just take your stuff, or leave it here if you prefer. What I'm trying to say is, the tenner really isn't that important. So only if you ever have the spare cash..."

I thought of asking my youngest aunt for some money. So I wrote her a letter explaining the gravity of the situation we were in, that I had a friend with me, and asked her to immediately send over some money.

Nevzat posted the letter himself.

While we waited for the money we were sure would arrive soon, we had nothing to do but wander around aimlessly, stare into shop windows, choose from among the luxury cars that drove by, and get into pointless arguments about which car was better. Gazi suggested that as soon as the money arrived, we should go and have ourselves a slap-up meal.

"No way!" I said, "Bread and cheese, and a bit of fruit. We have to make it last!"

"Is your aunt's husband rich?"

"Fairly..."

"Do they like you?"

"They used to..."

"A lot?"

"I guess so. 'You'll be the greatest doctor in Turkey,' they would say. So they must have liked me."

"Then there's nothing to worry about, is there? I'll bet they send you at least a hundred..."

"A hundred liras?"

"Sure! They'll think about what you'll need, and take into account that you have a friend with you. They'll not want you to be embarrassed in front of your friend. Don't you think?"

"Maybe... But maybe not."

"Don't think 'maybe not'! They care for you!"

"...?"

We were in Beyazit throughout this conversation,

sitting by the fountain. It was a warm, sunny day, and Istanbul was beautiful, but we were hungry!

"You know," I said, "it might be an idea to do another round of those restaurants..."

"Be patient," said Gazi, "don't abuse their goodwill. Look, Nevzat isn't kicking us out. Let's just grit our teeth for another couple of days, and see what happens."

"You just want to carry on staying there until he kicks us out, don't you? You never used to be like this in Adana."

"I'm still not like that... It's just that we're stuck now, aren't we?"

A tramp was walking past. He shouted across the road to someone he knew.

"Hey, Metroviceli!" With that, he ran across the road.

I suddenly had a blinding flash.

"Hang on a minute!" I said to Gazi, "You remember that friend we made at the Cretan's café? 'Soldier' Nejip: Nejip Metroviceli, he was!"

"Yeah, he was. Soldier Nejip. What was his address?"

"I think I remember it... Metroviceli, Nejip. Working at the docks he was, up the Golden Horn ..."

"That'll do," said Gazi, grabbing me by the arm, "Come on, let's go!"

Off we went. We eventually found the docks. We walked around all the tobacco warehouses there. And sure enough, by lunchtime, there was Nejip, standing in front of us, covered in a filthy brown layer. He stank of tobacco. He could not believe his eyes. He hugged me, hugged Gazi, then hugged me again. Then he went into the warehouse, and asked for a short break. He shoved us into the restaurant next to the warehouse, and told us to have ourselves a good meal first.

"I've got to get back now," he said, "but when you're finished here, you can wait for me at the café. I'll have a word, so don't pay for anything!"

Gazi had already sat down.

"Don't just stand there," he said to me, "sit down, and let's tuck in!"

He impatiently tapped his fork on his plate.

"Let's not get too carried away," I suggested, "because..."

"Leave me alone. I'm so hungry, I can't see straight. Waiter, excuse me, over here... These waiters are a bit dozy... Hey, waiter, over here!"

The waiter came over.

"First," said Gazi, "bring me some cold dolma... Or, no, wait. I'll have hot dolma, but make sure the chef gives me some big ones!"

The waiter chuckled as he went off.

"What are you staring at?" Gazi asked me, "I'm going to eat a week's worth. What's it to you? But how did Nejip know we were hungry? Do we look that starved, I wonder? But that's what you call a friend. One look at us, and he could tell we were hungry. Good on him!"

The waiter brought his dolma.

"I'll have a bowl of soup, please." I said.

Nejip came over much later, when his shift was done. The streets were full of tobacco workers and their hubbub. I would love to have been one of their rusty-brown, dirty, but nonetheless happy crowd.

Nejip kept asking us questions, laughing, and being happy.

"We can go and see some games. You wouldn't believe some of the matches they have. Which club are you going to go to? I'd say you should get yourselves into Fenerbahce. You see Fenerbahce..."

Gazi and I were exchanging glances, and smiling to ourselves.

"So, which hotel are you staying in?" Nejip asked, after we'd had God knows how many coffees. "Is it a nice, clean place?"

Gazi winked at me.

"Very clean," he said.

"Well, you can stay with me for tonight anyway. Come on then... Do we have to let the hotel know?"

"Not really," said Gazi, and then burst out laughing. "What hotel, mate? How would we be in a hotel? We've been lucky to have a floor to crash on!"

"Whose floor have you been crashing on?"

"We met this guy called Nevzat, we're on the floor in his room."

"He shovels coal for a living."

"And I thought that..." began Nejip, and then stopped. He started walking off, and beckoned to us to follow.

Well whatever he had thought, it didn't stop him being the perfect host.

We went along some streets, around a few corners, entered a crowded neighbourhood with lots of tiled roofs and bay windows, and then into his family's small wooden house. He led us into their sitting room. The house was shady and cool inside. A white, fleeting image of a woman flickered to and fro, first at one end of the room, then at the other.

The cover of the divan and the curtains in the sitting room had been delicately embroidered in greens and pinks and purples. There were no pictures on any of the walls: Only thickly framed large, ornate texts in Arabic.

"My mother won't allow photographs in this room," explained Nejip, "because she prays here."

The floorboards were yellow from years of polishing. I could see the side of a hill out of the window, occupied by a graveyard.

We respectfully kissed the wrinkled hands of Nejip's aging mother. She spoke a little Turkish. She asked us polite questions, as best she could, and we tried to provide answers. It was getting dark. Nejip's sister, who also worked in the tobacco warehouse, came into the room wearing blue earrings, and with her curly hair uncovered. "Welcome," she said, and went and lit the pink lamp on the sideboard before leaving us again. Before long we were joined by Nejip's dark-moustachioed father, his plaster-splattered uncle, and his elder brother, who turned out to be a carpenter. They all had thick and calloused hands, and chatted to us in their broken Turkish. I thought they were wonderful people, particularly the father. He talked about things, smoothed his thick moustache in an authoritative manner, and swore frequently. Meanwhile Nejip's sister lay out the dining cloth across the floor, put the chopping board down, lay down the little flannels we would be using as napkins, and brought in the bread-box. She did all this as if playing a little game, smiling now and then, and revealing a sparkling gold tooth whenever she did so. I wondered who she was smiling for: Me or Gazi?

After we had eaten our meal, drunk our coffees, and chatted about things of no consequence, we finally retired to the beds Nejip's sister hade made up for us. Our beds had been laid out side by side. All the bedding was spotlessly clean, expertly patched here and there, and smelled of soap.

We climbed into our beds.

"Ahhh..." I sighed, "This is great!"

Gazi lifted his head up.

"What?" he asked, "You mean the girl? I could get engaged to her immediately!"

I got very cross with him.

"You unscrupulous..."

"No, that's what you are! Now, I know that if I don't beat you to it..."

"What?"

"Come on, I saw you. Giving her all those leery looks."

The next morning we had a marvellous breakfast, and wandered down to Galata. The day passed.

"Once this money from your aunt comes through," said Gazi, on the day after that, "we can invite Nejip out."

"Yes, that'll be good. We can take him out for a meal."

"To a decent place. With raki, and proper meze."

"We'll pay back Nevzat too."

"Obviously. We'll also have to invite him out as well."

"We could do that, you know. Take him along to a restaurant with Nejip. We ought to, really."

"We could order two full bottles of raki…"

"If I get about a hundred and fifty or so, then it really won't matter."

"I wouldn't worry. Your aunt's bound to send you at least that. Because she does know you have a friend with you as well…"

That evening, Nevzat handed me the letter I had long been waiting for. I excitedly ripped open the envelope. Gazi and I leaned over as one, and quickly read the brief note.

I was to leave any so-called friend and come over right away. There would be no need for me to pay the bus fare – I had only to give my uncle's name. And when was I going to learn not to let every bum and scrounger tag along wherever I went!

Gazi had changed colour. I tore up the letter, and threw it out of the side window and into the smell of fried fish. First, we sold my clothes, and then my suitcase.

"Istanbul is one of a kind!"

You can hop off its trams, hop onto its taxis, and entertain who you want at the restaurant of your choice… You can set up a factory, or stay unemployed, or open a bank… Whatever you want!

"Istanbul is one of a kind!"

Then what?

Well then, it was first one bit of work, then another. We worked as waiters in cafés around Galata, shovelled coal, did a bit of street selling, and occasionally played for some of the useless local football teams, all for no more than a square meal.

"Istanbul is one of a kind!"

Then finally one morning, half starving, we bade farewell to the bridge, to the trams, to the dirty sea, to Galata, and to Pera, and boarded a ship back home,

leaving all those beautiful women to the men of Istanbul.
Farewell, then, Istanbul!

VIII

We saw Hasan Hussein the very night we got back to
Adana. We found out that my girl had got together with a
sailor. Gazi's had got engaged to her cousin, who worked
as a farm-hand in a nearby village, and the Cretan café
owner had been busted for dealing dope, and was doing
time.

"How about that?" mused Gazi, "Would you believe
it?"

As for me…

"What are you thinking?" Hasan Hussein asked me.

"Don't mind him," said Gazi, "he just can't let things
go. I don't know what it is with him — you can't dwell on
these things…"

It was nearly midnight by the time I left Gazi and
Hasan Hussein. I went over to the old sycamore tree,
where we used to light matches and signal our girlfriends.
The old sycamore was waiting patiently, looking resigned
to whatever fate may bring. I leaned back against it. Over
in the distance I saw the two brightly-lit windows. It all
looked exactly the way we had left it. I gave a loud
whistle. I noticed the shadows pause at one of the
windows, listening out. My second whistle created more
of a commotion. Then, one of the shadows climbed on the
sofa. The lamp signalled "Coming!" My face started to
twitch, and my left ear suddenly started hum. I thought of
how she would break down and apologise… How on earth
was she going to explain what she had done to me? How, I
wondered, how???

She arrived, and stood in front of me without even
saying 'Welcome back'. We stood silently for a while.

"Is it true?" I asked, eventually.

She kept silent.

"So it is true?"

Still nothing.

"How did you meet him?" I asked.

She still didn't say anything.

"So," I said, "I don't have a chance?"

She raised her head and looked up to the stars, then crossed her arms in front of her chest.

"There's no way he could love you the way I do," I said, "you're going to regret this, believe me. You're really going to regret it."

She shrugged.

I flicked away the last of my cigarette, and walked back.

Back on the tarmac, I walked under the electric lights, hearing the occasional whistle of a night-watchman. As I went around one corner, someone caught up with me and grabbed me by the arm. I looked, it was Hasan Hussein.

"Is all this nonsense over now?" he asks.

I couldn't bring myself to say 'It's over'.

"Hey, I'm asking you.. Is it all over?"

"But, you see..."

"Look mate. There are no ifs or buts left anymore. You've got to get your act together. You've either got to go back to school, or get yourself a proper job."

"Got a light?"

I lit a cigarette.

IX

"I'd expect stray dogs in the street to show more common sense than you do!" declared my grandmother.

If only I had left my friend and stayed at my aunts. In this harsh world, it was each man for himself. Blah blah blah.

Gazi got a major beating from his dad. Obviously, because he went along with some no-good bum and ran away from home!

Three days later, he was forced to start work at a flour mill his uncle had in a nearby village. And about two weeks after that, my mother turned up with my sisters. She carried stern orders from my father.

He had said that I shouldn't have left school in the first place, and that I must decide on what to do with my life...

"OK," I said, "I'll go to school."

"'OK I'll go to school'?" said my mother, shocked, "Aren't you going to school now?"

My grandmother took over, and went on and on. She ended up where she had started:

"The dogs in the street have more brains..."

My mother looked at me anxiously.

I knew my parents had moved over to Jerusalem after I'd left. From what my mother was saying, they were living in terrible poverty there. They were living in one small, dilapidated room in a large building full of Bedouin tribesmen. Niyazi had suddenly shot up, but he was very skinny. He apparently walked the streets of Jerusalem all day long, selling bits and pieces from a tray. And if only he could walk the streets in peace: He wasn't Palestinian, so he had to stay clear of the British police, as did all the foreigners there.

Once, a policeman chased him. Niyazi ran, and the policeman ran after him. Just then, a tram went by. Niyazi jumped in one door, out of the other, and fell over. His tray broke, all his good scattered, his palms scraped along the ground, and he was left covered in blood.

My mother was both laughing and crying as she told the story.

"Isn't life strange? We hoped to bring him up so carefully, like a delicate flower, trying to shield him from everything... At his age, he shouldn't have to be working or worrying about money. He should be going to school. Mind you, it's not as if children even younger don't work, but still, when it's your own flesh and blood..."

I thought of Niyazi. We once sat side by side on the edge of the fountain outside our Beirut home, measuring our legs with string so that we could establish whose were the thicker. Both of us had had long, skinny legs and knobbly knees. Mine had pale, light hair, whereas his were darker.

"And what about all the fighting between the Arabs and the Jews?" asked my mother.

Not a day went past without people being killed, or shops set alight; particularly on days when they had curfew. Apparently on such days my father would pace up and down their building and get annoyed at anything and everything. He always wanted Niyazi to be back a good hour or so before curfew started, but Niyazi inevitably got back just as the curfew started, or with only a matter of minutes to spare, carrying his tray. My father would shout and get annoyed. Apparently Niyazi would then just quietly go to the room.

"Didn't Niyazi want to come over with you?" I asked my mother.

"Of course he did," she said, "he'd even got his passport ready."

"And?"

"The last evening he was laughing and messing with his sisters. He was telling them all about the things he would do when he got to Adana. How little Memet's brother would be surprised to see him, how he was going to go back to school, play football again... He was so excited! But then, I don't know what came over him. In the morning, he'd suddenly changed his mind. And his father had insisted too..."

I didn't need to ask why. He wasn't as self-centred as I was...

"Whatever I do," my mother said, "I must find some money from somewhere to send over to them!"

We had some fields that had been taken into "administrative security" by the government after my father had fled, and these were now being unlawfully used by the neighbouring landowners. My mother was going to try and get these back, go to court if necessary, get the surveyors there to establish the borders of our land, and then find people to rent the land to, and then…

"It won't be easy," said my grandmother, "You think I haven't tried? All through the winter, the storms, in and out of knee-deep mud… There was this one time… I went and saw that man… That Abdulfettah, Gulistan's husband, remember her? Her husband. You should see them now, putting on airs and graces. He used to come to package the tobacco… A man you wouldn't have considered worth talking to. But what can you do? Until you get what you want, you've got to humour them… Mind you, I gave him a piece of my mind, the horrible little man. My son sends his regards, I told him. I told him my son had told us 'Go find Abdulfettah, and he'll sort everything out. He'll get back all the fields for you, work the land along with his own, and give you a rightful share without you having to ask for a thing.' When I said that he just cowered in the corner listening to me, looking like a trapped pig. 'Oh madam,' he said, 'We can barely work our own fields. We couldn't possibly manage anyone else's… I wouldn't want to do wrong by you. As far as I know your fields are simply lying there empty. You should arrange for someone to work them!'"

"'Well then, sir,' I said to him, 'why is everybody telling me that our fields are being worked by Abdulfettah and his brother?'"

"You should have seen his reaction! He exploded, started having fits! 'Look here, my good woman,' he said, and started coming towards me…"

It seems my grandmother had taken particular offence at being called someone's 'good woman'.

So now, it was my poor mother's turn to try her luck.

"I have no choice," she said, "I have to talk to him, take him to court if I have to… The family's in terrible poverty." Then she turned to me.

"And you, young man, are going straight back to school!"

X

My mother really threw herself into the business with the fields. Written applications, title deeds, squatters' notices, Courts of Law... Days, weeks, months went by. The results were always inconclusive, and mother was getting tired. She would get back home late at night, drop the fat file of official papers, and throw herself down on the sofa. In order to save money, we sat in the dark. My mother's hair had rather suddenly turned white and, coupled with her sunken eyes, the sight of her depressed us all.

I had holes in the soles of my shoes, and the hems of my trouser legs were frayed. Most days I went to school without so much as a five kurus coin in my pocket. In spite of my father's strict orders, my yellow-striped school cap, and the incredible madhouse that was 3-B, going to school still didn't appeal to me, and the bond between me and my school weakened as time wore on.

I was no longer a child. While my brother and father were in appalling poverty, my now white-haired and sunken eyed mother struggled though knee-deep mud, and my sisters lost more weight all the time, it was clear to me that my secondary education was a luxury we couldn't afford. I felt I had no right to allow this to continue.

Our fair weather friends gradually deserted us. People no longer found pleasure in our company, and the things we talked about made others feel ill at ease.

"Why did my father have to do it? Did he think that he could single-handedly right the wrongs of the world? Look at what he's done to us, all for the sake of strangers... It's each man for himself out there..."

"Goodness me," said my mother, "You're forgetting what a respected man your father was! It wasn't that long ago that people like this wouldn't have been able raise their heads in his presence..."

Whatever anyone said, I was aware that we were in a very rapid decline. What were we going to hold on to? We were all alone, isolated in a mass of people who simply didn't care. People who shrugged, and thought only of themselves. There was certainly plenty of proof of this...

On one of the days when we didn't even have bread and black olives – that mainstay which was the last to depart from the poorest households – my mother went to ask a very close relative of ours for a small loan.

"I'll ask for at least ten liras," she said to me, "so I can manage to get some bread and olives, and maybe a little tea and sugar. It'll keep us going for a while. After that, we'll see what God's will is. If the girls wake up do keep them occupied, I'll try and get back as quickly as possible!"

We had gone to bed hungry the night before. My mother was late coming back. The girls woke up. They asked where mother was. I told them she had gone to get some bread and olives, and that she should be back any minute. They were delighted. Our youngest sister clapped her hands in excitement.

"Oh, good old mummy! I'm so hungry!"

It was a grey, damp morning. It had rained heavily earlier, and now there was a steady stream of water flowing down the roads.

Mother returned eventually. Her hands were empty. She looked completely drained and absolutely forlorn. She slowly started to climb the stairs. She managed to make it to the top, but just as she was about to go into her room she swayed. She held on to the doorframe.

"A little water..." she croaked, "Let me have a sip of water."

But before we could rush her a glass, she collapsed in front of the doorway.

What was going on?

The girls ran to get our landlady. Our landlady came along in her white headscarf, muttering prayers. She held my mother's wrist.

"Eau de Cologne!" she demanded.

We had none.

"A little floral infusion, perhaps, or even some vinegar?"

"...?"

"Don't you even have some vinegar?"

We don't have any, we don't have any, we don't have any! We don't have anything! This abject poverty was driving me mad, and the ground felt as if it were melting away from under my feet.

"Don't you even have some vinegar?"

"No, we don't even have some vinegar! We don't have a home, we don't have a car, we don't have any property, we don't have any land, and we don't even have any vinegar!"

My fists were planted firmly on my hips. Was it some great social wrong, this failure to own vinegar?

The landlady went away, and came back with some Eau de Cologne of her own. She brought my mother to. My mother stared around in confusion at first, her ashen face full of concern, then... She pulled her knees up, rested her forehead on them, and started sobbing uncontrollably. She cried and cried. And although we tried to find out, she did not tell us why she had fainted that day. We only found out much later that when she went to our relative, our close relative, she had been treated very badly. She hadn't even been asked in. They kept her at the street door as they asked her what she wanted. My mother told them. And this woman – a close, indeed very close relative – said:

"What's the point? There'll be no end to this."

She told my mother that my father shouldn't have been involved in politics, that everyone had to bear their responsibilities in life, and that he shouldn't have harmed his nearest and dearest for the sake of strangers. He should have been thankful for what he had, and looked after his family properly...

"But the children are hungry at home," pleaded my

mother, "I don't want to dredge up things from the past."

"Right," said this woman, this close, indeed very close relative, "so you don't want to dredge up the past either. Well then, let's both close the book on this whole sordid affair."

And slammed the street door in my mother's face.

XI

When I found this out, our dilapidated little room spun wildly around me. Should I go to that woman who 'closed the book' and burn their large mansion down, beat up her son, or just turn up at their door and create a complete scandal?

Could I really do all that?

Maybe...

But, I thought to myself, to what end? What would it solve?

A mansion might burn down, some kid might get beaten up, or maybe the madam would be mortified with embarrassment. So what? The end result was bound to be negative. Status quo, with the Law on its side, would not sympathise with a brave lad waving his fists at a cliff.

I realised that waving my fists at a cliff would be a pointless gesture.

....

Gazi was still at his uncle's mill and under strict control, Hasan Hussein was in the third year of the college of commerce, and I was at 3-B in my secondary school.

The girls were in 3-A, and the eldest ones were barely sixteen. What we had in 3-B was 'Hamlet' Saim, 'Pipe' Ziya, 'Black' Sadri, 'Bear' Mumtaz, 'Kurd' Sermet and the like, and even the youngest of us were old enough to have children of our own, were we to get married.

Yet when I looked around, I might see Bear Mumtaz drawing a caricature of our history teacher on the blackboard while Kurd Sermet pinned a paper tail to his backside. The class would roar and shout until Bear Mumtaz cottoned on, at which point he would start effing and blinding at whoever pinned the tail on him. Meanwhile Kurd Sermet, clutching his stomach, in pain from laughing so hard, would be ready to bolt away from any punishment Bear Mumtaz might decide to mete out. As soon as Bear Mumtaz realized who was responsible, we would get a chase across the tops of the desks, and the whole class would break out into a dusty riot. The shouts and guffaws, and the loud banging of the desk tops would last for some time, until the door would silently swing open, revealing the silhouette of a large and irate headmaster. The chaos would instantly come to an end. The whole class would be a frozen tableau of respect, smiles wiped clean off all our faces.

The head master would look around the class for a time, scrutinising each of us in turn.

"I have yet to decide," he would say, "on whether this is a class, a barn full of animals, or a den of criminals. Now listen to me boys... This sort of behaviour is totally unacceptable. Now, if you do insist on behaving like animals, I have to warn you that I will not hesitate in treating you as if you were."

But, we never were treated that way. At least, not while I was there.

I didn't take pleasure in any of the classroom antics, though... I just didn't feel involved. I kept thinking of my mother, my sisters, and particularly of my brother Niyazi, there with shredded knees from tumbling off the tram. If some of my family were in abject poverty there, and the rest were in abject poverty here, it seemed to me that this secondary school was an unaffordable luxury. You couldn't put education before food. I was feeling the burden of responsibility falling on my shoulders, and the feeling was intensifying by the day. What would a secondary school diploma give me anyway? Even if I got this piece of paper – and in those days, a secondary school diploma virtually guaranteed a job – who would be foolhardy enough to give 'that exiled man's son' a job in their department?

I had to start working, but doing what?

Should I go back to weaving again? Or do plain labouring on building sites? Should I do back-breaking farm work in the cotton fields, or during the harvest under that baking Chukurova sun?

It seemed to me that the easiest thing to do would be to become a fruit-seller. Selling melon, water-melon and grapes. Now that sounded good. Depending on the season, I might sell lemons, oranges, or sugar cane, or whatever. I'd be sure to earn a bit of a living. Well, of course I could earn a living. But in my home town? In front of all my friends and – in particular – in front all those people who were oh-so-clever and knew not to put the interests of strangers before that of one's own family? All those people thought of my father's principled life as some form of stupidity. But look at them. Having decided 'you only live once', they wanted to dress well, eat well, travel, enjoy themselves... They had no interest in why many other people weren't able to do the same. They wanted the wheels to keep turning the way they always had. And they couldn't care less about what enabled those wheels to turn...

I felt I carried this immense burden of shame, with my holed shoes and frayed trousers. A stupid father would have a stupid son. The standard by which we were judged was their standard. By that standard I was stupid, and ugly, and pathetic. Therefore I had to escape from them, to hide, to remain out of sight with my holed shoes and frayed trousers. I felt uncomfortable when I walked on past their disapproving stares and snide whispers.

This aspect of my personality developed rapidly. I started to feel embarrassed about my hooked nose, my withered hands, and my gaunt face. Whenever I felt people staring at me my hair would stand on end, and I'd get a cold and uncomfortable feeling creeping down inside me. My ears would hum, my vision would blur, my hands would go cold and clammy, and I'd feel as if I was shrinking, and that my hooked nose was curving down even more, and that I was becoming an even uglier monstrosity.

After a time, I started to feel uncomfortable even when I walked past shop displays. It was as if all the shiny new things for sale were specifically for those people who dressed well, ate well, and travelled. I felt that when I got too close, the items on display would glare at me disapprovingly. So I ended up avoiding them, and staying clear of all those attractive, shiny new items on display.

It had all been so easy when I was a kid. Was this what growing up was all about? It felt as if all around me was now dark. I wanted to see a light at the end of the tunnel; I wanted to feel that there was a way out. I wanted a complete change. I did not want anyone to look down on me, even if I sold melon, worked in a factory, went around with holed shoes or frayed trousers. I didn't want anyone to look on disapprovingly. I didn't want people to give me dirty looks because of my hooked nose or my spindly hands.

But there was no chance of that.

In time, the disdainful looks and the snide remarks made me withdraw into my shell, like a pathetic little snail. So I took to going out of town, and spending my time in empty fields.

The fields! The open air!

Yet I felt unable to fully appreciate the beauty of the blue sky, arching like a giant dome over knee-deep green covered fields, framing a space filled with buzzing bees and fluttering butterflies, and with the sparrows and doves chasing around in the bright sunshine. I knew I didn't have to withdraw into my shell, like a snail, but I felt as if fate was conspiring against me.

I'd often lie on my back on the grass, stare at the

passing wispy clouds, and wonder about God's mysterious ways.

It was God who saw even the tiniest step of the tiniest dark ant, even if it was walking on a dark piece of ground in complete darkness, and it was He who had ordained at the very start of time that it be so. He was the Ruler of our fate, the Master of the universe, and the Creator of both good and evil, and of the devil. What did he want from our family? Why had my father gone into politics and been on the losing side, why had we ended up in poverty, having to go around with holed shoes and frayed trousers, why was I the target of disdain from all those around me?

It was clearly because God, He who saw even the tiniest step of the tiniest ant, He who was the Ruler of our fate and the Master of our universe; He had ordained right at the very start of time that this was to be our fate. This was clearly the case. But why? What evil had we done to deserve such a fate, as ordained by Him? Why the disdainful looks? I had no say over my own fate. And if He was actually on their side, it would be appalling...

One day, seeking answers to all my questions, I raised my head to His blue skies.

"What are You trying to tell me?" I asked, "Tell me, why are You doing this? Why? Where's the justice in it? It just doesn't seem right. What do You want from us? You're laughing at us, aren't You? Just like the others, You're laughing at us!"

I never would find out whether God actually heard my words, or whether he laughed at me or not. But I could see that I was like a scorpion surrounded by a ring of fire. If I walked the paved roads of the city I would be in the ring of fire, created by those who thought they were here on earth only to eat plenty and travel afar. Yet when I threw myself into the open fields, I was in the ring of fire made by God. I had no third place to escape to.

Then I started watching the ants. I admired the endless hard work these tiny animals were capable of. I felt inspired by their collective will, as they united in vast numbers and moved a dead earthworm.

If only I could be an ant... Anyway, what was He up to? Why make me human, make them ants, and make the others flies, horses, elephants, tigers or fish?

64

....

Hours would go by. The clouds would acquire a pink tinge, and the sweaty labourers would return from the vineyards. No matter how long I thought about things, it made no difference. I had no chance of solving the riddles of creation. Just as I thought I might be approaching an answer, I'd see another impossible conundrum and, under the now dark skies, I would feel deflated. I would then helplessly start making my way back to the city, and to that ring of fire, my arms dangling hopelessly by my sides.

I did occasionally pop in to school. One day the headmaster called me, Kurd Sermet and Bear Mumtaz to his study, to give us an earful about our absences. He had the three of us lined up, but it was me he was staring at most.

"As for you," he ended up saying, "especially you, number one hundred and thirty-six, you are the worst!"

I had my eyes lowered to the ground and felt dizzy. My ears were buzzing. Me, number one hundred and thirty-six, especially me. The chick thrown out of the nest, the fruit too bitter for even the frost to spoil. Why am I still staying in this ring of fire? What did I expect from them? Their 'easy money' certificate? Among these people all I am is a snail, having to shrivel up in his shell and stay there, right?

Leave their diplomas to them, I decided, I'll go and do my own thing.

So I quit school.

XII

When I announced I had quit school, my mother cried for a long time.

"Oh my God!" she wailed, "This is exactly what I feared most! Do my sons have to become little men, obliged forever to kowtow to others? Oh, to think of all the high hopes I had!"

I felt indignant.

"I shall never kowtow to anyone," I announced, "not for anything!"

I felt a load lift off me, as if I had finally made a gap in the ring of fire. I felt as if my father and Niyazi were looking on approvingly.

"Well done son," I imagined my father saying, "You've finally given up on building castles in the air while the family is starving."

"So, now you've quit school and you haven't got a job either," my mother said a few days later, "You might as well start running around and try and sort out all this business with our fields!"

She was right. My mother was absolutely right, but those fields... Rain, knee-deep mud, nettles in the summer, the dirty tracks of the village, irate hounds, and that man Abdulfettah, with his ruddy face and grey-blue eyes, calling my grandmother his 'good woman'!

What if he chased me too?

"You're a man!" my mother said, "They're going to think twice before trying anything with you. After all, I'm only a woman!"

One morning, in the dark purple pre-dawn haze, I joined the queue at the minibus-stop and about twenty of us piled into this ten-seater, creaky old minibus. We headed off to the crow-ridden town where I'd been born. I was going to the old farm for the first time in years! I wondered who I'd see there: Would I see Madam Selem, who had helped us through long winter nights, tucked us in our cosy beds, and sent shivers down our spines with her tales of the King of the fairies, of genies, and of the emerald-green Phoenix; tales full of snakes, centipedes, and wise old exorcists? The snotty son of the daily who taught us to eat raw aubergine? Or perhaps the chicken Niyazi and I had hung from branches in our attempts to train them?

The inside of the minibus stank of feet, garlic and cheese. I felt the weight of Abdulfettah's steely blue-eyed stare on me.

The minibus was clanking and creaking along, rounding bends, and somehow managing to stay up under its load. There was no lid on its radiator; it had been replaced with a lump of wood, and steam escaped angrily from the small gaps around its edges.

I kept my eyes on the kilometer marker stones. I had done this route so often with my father. My father would be at the wheel, and I'd be sitting next to him. Every so often he'd get me to hold the steering wheel, so that he could light a cigarette. While he was preoccupied with lighting his cigarette, I would quickly pull down the advance and acceleration levers as far as they would go. The car would suddenly shoot forward at an incredible speed. Suddenly aware of his surroundings, my father would anxiously grab the steering wheel back, and pull up both the advance lever and the acceleration lever.

"You idiot!" he'd yell, "You'll flip the car over!"

The roads were still all the same roads, and the kilometer markers hadn't changed. Over in the distance stood the same ancient mountains, rising up in waves and peaks. Finally the old town appeared in the distance, at first little more than a long, dark, horizontal strip. We were getting closer. As we entered the town, we were almost scraping against the sun-baked walls flanking the narrow road. Our minibus hobbled along the unevenly paved street, managed to reach the taxi rank, and juddered to a halt. I jumped off. My feet were numb. I headed off towards the market-place. My hands were in my pockets, touching the few coins I had. No one paid a blind bit of notice to my holed shoes, my frayed trousers, my hooked nose, my bony hands or my gaunt face. Not a single person so much as glanced in my direction. This was real freedom. I loved the people of this town now, these lovely people who ignored me.

I passed the Albanian's open-air café on my left. I remember my father's red, nineteen twenty-seven model Ford would be parked right there in front of the café, and the young Arab who looked after the car would be there too, holding his spanner, tightening this or that or cleaning the sparkplugs, and my father would have sat just there, or perhaps there, talking to his friend, the bearded retired general, discussing wheat, barley or cotton prices, and doing calculations on the back of his cigarette box with a pencil. They would look at each other now and then, smile, and wink knowingly. The red-bearded general was a hard, harsh man. He would always move his arms around, describing huge arcs as he talked.

He would transfix us all with his amazing tales from our War of Liberation.

But sometimes he and my father would talk of things which did not interest me in the slightest. I would stretch and yawn, and stare past the café door at the painting of a noble horseman inside and get lost in that, or re-count the number of posts holding up the wooden framework outside the café.

I was comfortable walking down this road. I went past the café, and then past the grocer's, the barber's and other cafés... I realised I knew the stationer, standing over by the fountain. I recognised the man, but there was no way he could possibly recognise me. He was a flat-headed man from Turkistan. When we were being schooled in the mosque by the market-place, we would go to his damp, dank shop to get our books, pencils and paper. He was also the local stockist of the "Anatolian Child's Primer".

Back in those days, they had taught us a marching song which had been written and composed by General Kazim Karabekir. They would take us on long marches, and make us sing it all the way.

Arms of steel
Feet of bronze
Will Turks yield?
Will Turks yield?

Turks ne'er yield
Turks ne'er yield
Come what may
Turks ne'er yield

As I slowly walked down the road, I felt so relaxed... I was softly singing the parts of the march I still remembered:

Army of Greeks
Crawling worms
Will Turks yield?
Will Turks yield?

Turks ne'er yield
Turks ne'er yield
Come what may
Turks ne'er yield

We had a short, dark, rotund teacher, who would lead our troop, march to our tempo, and sweat like a pig. Red dye from his Fez would bleed with his sweat, run down his forehead and cheeks, and make the man look like a clown. We would crack up. I remember once...

Suddenly, I heard my name being called. Oh no, not someone else I know? I turned to see. Yes, it's someone I know alright. And how! The man knew not only my father, but my grandfather too. This was the man who, years ago, came over to our farm, talked of the commotion in the cities, and counted the grains on one spike of wheat. A former Member of the High Court!

It turned out that he now had a hardware store. He invited me to his store. He offered me a chair, and ordered us coffees. He studied me in minute detail. I was being inspected in a friendly and warm manner but, not having had such close attention for years, I felt quite uncomfortable. My hands and face felt clammy again, and I was sure my nose had become even more crooked. What if he notices that my trousers are frayed?

I kept avoiding his gaze. I found it difficult to accept that the eyes looking at me may be friendly. I was withdrawing into my shell, occasionally sticking my head out insecurely. I thought he might say, "What a skinny, ugly child! His father was so good-looking too…"

In fact, he was only chatting to me pleasantly. He spoke of my father's childhood, of my uncle who had died of tuberculosis, of my aunts, of the sweets one could get in the old days, and of the dos and celebrations that followed the fasting at Ramadan. I slowly let my head extend out from my shell. I seemed to be warming to the man; the wall between us was getting lower. I started to relax.

"You're not like your father, though!" he announced suddenly. "The great man couldn't get through your normal doorway. You're all skinny!"

I immediately withdrew into my shell again, and the wall between us crept back up. I started to feel a chill on my face and hands, and a slight twitch in my left eye.

His next question came down like a second blow.

"I take it you finished high-school?"

Oh no! I started to feel overwhelmed by my own feelings of worthlessness. I was certainly the ugliest, skinniest person in the world. What if he finds out that not only had I not finished high-school, but that I hadn't even made it halfway, and finished middle-school?

I didn't know how to reply.

"Let's go over to my house," he continued, "and let the wife see you. She'll be surprised to see how you've grown!"

One disaster after another! He didn't even give me time to come up with some excuse for not going. He picked up his walking stick and his felt hat, and we left the store.

"You're being rather reserved my boy," he said to me, "I not only knew your father, I knew your grandfather! There's no reason to feel uncomfortable. Your father, now, he was such a man…"

I was following him from behind, a little to his left. I was trying to adjust my youthful steps to match his slow gait. I felt I had a diffident air about me, and the image of my mother floated in front of me.

"Look at yourself!" she was saying to me, "You have turned into someone who kowtows to others!"

I shook myself. I undid the buttons on my jacket, and opened up my steps. I drew level the man. My mother disappeared. No sooner than I had got rid of that load, I realised that I had no right to be walking by his side. After all, he was a member of the High Court, and there I was, not even a middle-school graduate!

I fell back a little and buttoned up my jacket. My mother came back…

We finally arrived at his house. It was a two-storey, solid house built of stone. He smartly raised and lowered the door-knocker twice in succession, in a very "proper" manner. I heard the shuffling of slippers behind the door. The door opened. An elderly lady, tightly wrapped in her white headscarf, peered out before withdrawing back. We entered, and the woman pulled back further. The man was cackling to himself knowingly.

"See if you can recognise the young man, dear!" he says.

The woman, conditioned by Islam, was clearly nervous as she raised her eyes to look up at a stranger.

"Well dear," she says, "I'm not sure… He seems a bit familiar, but…"

The noise of a fractious young child and of a young woman calming it came from the room next door.

"Come on, you know who it is!"

There I was, standing with an impatient old man, and a confused old lady who was staring at me. The reassuring lullaby suddenly ceased.

"Shadiye, girl!" he called out, "Leave the child and come here a minute!"

Oh dear! I shrivelled up under my shell again. I knew that the young mother about to join us would be taken aback by my sheer ugliness. I was ashamed, ashamed, ashamed. My trousers were all frayed, my shoes had holes...

"Yes, father?"

A pair of jet-black eyes, an ever-so-white face, and a tangle of hair.

My heart was pounding. I felt a warm rush of blood to my face. Her white headscarf had slipped down onto her shoulders, revealing too much, and I noticed her firm bosoms, her full chest... I saw no possibility of this young woman finding anything appealing about me.

"Your mother didn't recognise him. I want to see if you do!"

The young mother could only have been around my age. She was not inhibited in the slightest. She inspected my face closely. The hook of my nose stung like an open wound. I assumed she thought "What an ugly person!"

"Well, to be honest, father, I'm not sure..."

"Hah!" exclaimed the old man, "I recognised him the moment I set eyes on him!"

He explained.

The elderly lady, who had so far been cowering slightly because of this "stranger" standing next to her, undid her scarf in obvious relief.

"Goodness me, look at you!" she said, "To think that I thought... My, my. You have grown, haven't you?"

Then she turned to her husband.

"He doesn't look like his father, does he?"

"No he doesn't. You couldn't get his father through a doorway!"

I felt as if I was floundering in open space, falling endlessly. Oh, my skinniness, my hooked nose, my withered hands, my lack of education, oh my this, my that, my the other...

They asked me all sorts of questions about my father, my mother, my aunts... Shadiye had gone into the kitchen to cook up some eggs with pastrami, and we sat in their dining room, at the table, by the light of their gas-lamp, talking. Well, I wasn't talking so much as being questioned.

The food arrived, and we started eating. I moved in all sorts of ridiculous ways so that Shadiye didn't see my withered hands. In my haste I let things drip and missed my mouthfuls. Occasionally, our eyes met. How I wished I was the most handsome man in the world!

"Our Shadiye," explained the old man, "has been widowed at a young age, and with a young child too!"

So-and-so's son had shot the old man's son-in-law last winter, over some land dispute.

The fact that she was a widow gave me some hope. There was no escaping the fact that I had many shortcomings. But on the other hand, she was a widow. If she liked me, and we got married... Well, I'd never beat her child. But how could we? There I was, unwaged, ugly, holes in my shoes, frayed trousers, uneducated... Could it work?

My eyes went to my withered hands for the umpteenth time. I pulled them back off the table, and rested them on my lap, hiding them.

"What's up my boy?" the old man asked, "You've got to eat... Look at you, you're all skin and bones!"

I stiffened. I felt as if I had been whacked with a stick in my most sensitive spot. Right in front of Shadiye, too. How could he? I would have run out of their house right then and there, except it would have been terribly ill-mannered. A cold feeling oozed out of my forehead.

Then the old woman whispered a question to her husband.

"No, he hasn't!" said the man, "He hasn't even

finished high-school!"

Oh, the value these people attached to their 'easy-money' certificate!

"What about middle school?" asked his wife.

"Well, he's bound to have finished middle school!"

They turned to look at me. I had to somehow end this line of conversation.

"Sir, did you ever read 'Two Friends Travel the World'?"

The old man looked surprised at first.

"I can't say I have." he said, "So tell me, young man, what do you do? Do you have a job somewhere? Maybe we could find you something around here. You can't simply walk around doing nothing, you know. Bring your middle-school diploma with you when you're next here, and we'll try and arrange something with the local authority, hmm?"

This was as much as I could take.

"Did you say job?" I said, raising my head firmly, "Thank you, but no. I have taken a Bank Clerks' exam… I'll be starting in a few days."

The man was surprised.

"Oh? Well done. Well, then…"

"Yes, indeed."

"At a bank, you say?"

"Yes, at a bank."

"So high school graduates didn't take the exam, then?"

"There were twenty of us in the exam. Five were high-school graduates, and three were fully-fledged accountants."

"Well done! And I had thought that…"

He had thought that this emaciated, ugly, shy middle-school graduate was worthless. What did he know? Now I had fired the starting gun, I was going to run for all it's worth!

"I came here to sort out our fields. We have lots of fields, but a few of them are being occupied illegally at the moment. I'm here to sort those out. In fact, we don't really need the income from them all. There isn't really the need for me to work, with all that money coming in, but I thought I'd get a job anyway. You know, better than being idle... It seems there's this man Abdulfettah. He was particularly rude to my grandmother, I'm going to go and deal with him. I deliberately put on my old shoes and frayed trousers for this trip. I mean, obviously, I have plenty of shoes and clothes to choose from really."

How I made it all up! How important was a banking exam, under the circumstances?

"I shall be taking the Baccalaureate, and I shall then attend university. Later, I may take the European exams."

The old man winked at his wife.

"Oh, that's so good. What an intelligent and keen young man!"

"Just like his father, hmm?" said the woman.

I looked at Shadiye with pride. I thought she rather fancied me, and my bravado had reached the level of insolence.

Then we adjourned next door. The room had white curtains, white covers on the divan, a walnut crib, a laundry box decorated in yellow tin, and dresses hanging from the walls Shadiye started to breast-feed her baby. Occasionally she lifted her head up and smiled at me. I felt very confident now. I was managing to bravely return her looks. I felt warm murmurings inside me. Finally, her father said he was going to the café and left. I really relaxed then. I started telling her all sorts of things.

I pulled out a cinema magazine from my pocket, and Shadiye came and sat next to me. We looked at the pages together. Occasionally our heads would touch lightly, causing sparks to fly. We stared at a picture of an actress in a swimming costume. Her mother was on the divan, and had already started to snore. I edged a little closer to Shadiye, and then closer still. The side of my arm touched her swollen breast. I felt as if I was burning there. I was quivering, and my eyes were aflame. Suddenly I dropped the magazine, and put my arm around her waist.

She flipped out of my embrace like a large fish, and ran over to her baby's crib.

"You impudent little man!" she snapped, angrily.

My delicate self-confidence shattered completely. I immediately withdrew into my shell again, and shrivelled up. The wall rose between us. My hooked nose, my holed shoes, my withered hands, my gaunt features and my frayed trousers all came back to haunt me. So did my mother.

"Oh, darling! Oh my poor dear!" she was saying.

Shadiye had literally turned her back on me, and wasn't even looking. What should I do? Should I get up and leave? No, that wouldn't do. Her father would ask why I left, and she would tell him everything, wouldn't she? But if I stayed... What would I do here?

What if she tells her mother? 'That dreadful man, he did this and he did that' she might say. And what if her mother then says to her father, 'Do you know what that awful boy was doing to your daughter?'

I felt totally out of place. I was in a terrible quandary. But just then her mother woke up and sat up, rubbing her eyes. The daughter turned to me, glaring with hatred. I prayed to God that she wouldn't tell her mother. The old woman and I went upstairs. She quickly made my bed, bade me goodnight, and left me.

How could I have a good night?

The window of the bedroom overlooked the street so I gazed out, absent-mindedly sucking on a finger, thinking all manner of things. There was an ice-cold moon in the sky. Rows of wet houses huddled together. Yellow lanterns illuminated the frozen silence.

What if she told her mother? And what if her mother then said to her father: 'Do you know what that young man of yours was up to? If you insist on bringing home tramps off the street...'

I imagined that the old man would listen to it all sadly, and comment on how times have changed, how children were no longer like their fathers, or their fathers' fathers.

"But," I kept saying to myself, "will the girl actually say anything to her mother?"

She may, or she may not. How could I tell? I took a five kurus coin out of my pocket. If she's going to tell, give me heads, and if she isn't, give me tails!

I shook the coin in my cupped hands, threw it in the air, and it landed heads. So she was going to tell! In which case, she must have done so by now. Her mother was probably just waiting for her father to get back home. But wait, how could I be so sure? I tossed the coin again. Heads again!

I was now certain. The girl must have told her mother. And her mother would tell her father. Heads, twice in a row!

I suddenly thought of God again, and the fate He had ordained. God had clearly ordained all of this right back at the beginning of time, I thought. This is why this was all happening. He had ordained one fate for me, and another for Shadiye. We were each on our own separate paths, obviously.

But forget about fate, and what God ordained, I thought; I was going to be a disgrace to the whole family. What could I do? I could quietly sneak down the stairs, listen at their door, and try and hear what they're saying. But what if Shadiye or her mother suddenly came out, and caught me like that?

Two heads in a row, she's bound to have told! And the mother... Well, she's just waiting for the old man. When he hears about it, he's going to say 'Shame on you. I treated you like a human being, and I let you into my home... And look at how you behaved.'

I was still by the window. Bats were silently fluttering in the air, looking a silvery-grey in the moonlight. I heard an owl hoot in the distance, and assumed that the folks in the thatched brick houses were fast asleep.

I got undressed and got into bed.

How could I possibly get to sleep?

Two heads, so she must have told. What am I to do now?

I covered my head with the quilt, and felt even worse. When I closed my eyes, my gaze was directed inwards. The inner me and I started a conversation.

"What will you do if she tells?"

"Heads came up, so she's going to. In fact, she probably already has."

"You think so?"

"She would have, by now."

"How do you know?"

"I got heads twice..."

"You always end up doing something to make matters worse!"

"Why did you attack the woman?"

"Was that really uncalled for?"

"More than simply uncalled for!"

"Well, it's done now."

"And you'll just have to suffer the consequences. They let you into their home out of respect for your family. How quickly you forgot that! Who do you think you are anyway? You're nobody. You've have neither the looks nor the money to amount to anything. What amazing quality did you imagine they saw in you? ... And what was all that about a banking exam anyway? You've no shame, have you? All those barefaced lies..."

"...!"

"What if they see grandmother one day, and one of them says something like 'We saw your grandson, and he told us all about his banking exam. How is his job going?' What would grandmother say? 'What bank? What exam? Him, work in a bank? He's been lying to you, bragging. Stray dogs have more sense than he does!' she'd say, wouldn't she?"

"…?"

"So then the old man would say, 'Oh, is that so? To think that we invited him into our home out of respect for you, and we fed him, put him up… And all he did was molest my daughter…' Wouldn't your grandmother make your world a living hell? Hmm? Don't go all quiet on me now! Answer me!"

....

When I woke up there was a silvery light in the sky, but it didn't look like morning.

My struggle with myself flared up again.

"The woman would have said something ages ago!"

"About what?"

"That matter…"

"Are we back to that again?"

"We are, because the woman will have told her husband. She would have given him all the details. The old man would have felt let down at first, and then he would have got mad. 'That tramp! That scoundrel! That shameless…' He won't have slept for hours, smoking cigarette after cigarette, getting more and more irate, waiting for me to show my face in the morning…"

"You really think so?"

"I know so."

"What are we going to do?"

"If you ask me, we should get up, get dressed, and get out of here!"

"But it's not even dawn yet. It's still dark out!"

"All the better. We couldn't make it out in the morning; the old man would be ready and waiting."

"So we should get out soon?"

"Immediately. Right now."

"But…"

"Don't waste time thinking about it. We have to go right now. Or else…"

I got out of bed, feeling the sudden cold, and quickly got dressed. I was shaking: my hands, the muscles of my face, all over. I was petrified that I would be caught, and things would become even worse. I carefully opened the bedroom door, and tiptoed over to the sofa. The white walls looked on sadly. As I tiptoed down the stairs, I noticed the knob on the end of the banisters. It was glaring at me angrily. The doorknobs downstairs, the corners of the walls, the windows, all the furniture had come to life, and they were all very angry. They looked as if they might scream out loud and attack me at any moment.

Shaking with nerves, I quickly opened the front door, slipped out, and hurried off without even closing the door behind me.

It was freezing cold outside. The streets were muddy, and there was a deathly stillness in the frozen light of the moon. I rapidly walked away from the house, turned a few corners, and made my way along the narrow, crooked, squelchy streets. The muddy water had entered my shoes from the holes in their bottom. I was turning so many corners, and going along so many little streets, I didn't know where I was. I didn't know the small town that well, and now I was completely lost I was afraid I would come across a night watchman. A watchman might ask where I was coming from, where I was headed, and what I was doing out in the streets at this hour. What would I say? What hotel's name could I give? He'd think I was a thief, or a fugitive from some prison, and take me straight down to the station. The truth would come out there, of course. Word would be sent to my grandfather's friend, and the old man would come rushing over. He would have been livid to start with, and then this would have happened on top of everything else.

"That's him alright," he'd say as soon as he stormed in, even as he was trying to get his breath back, "You know who he is? He's so-and-so's son! You wouldn't believe it, would you? No... I thought him a decent young man at first. I let him into my house, left him alone with my own wife and daughter. But do you know what he did...?"

What would I say? They would lock me up. And my mother, my grandmother, all our relatives, the woman who slammed the door in my mother's face, and then my father, all my home town, the whole planet would know I'd been arrested. I would just die. My grandmother would have a field day. "I told you, didn't I?" she would say, "Didn't I tell you that stray dogs have more sense?"

They'll say "He looks shifty. I bet he's a murderer," and who knows what else.

I suddenly noticed the shadow of a large watchman at the far end of the street, and hurriedly retraced my steps. I was in a state of panic. They were bound to catch up with me any second now, and take me straight down to the station.

I went around one corner, then the next. Then I heard the watchmen blowing their whistles. The shrill noises started coming from behind, then from in front of me as well, and from either side. I was going mad. It was as if all the watchmen of the town had realised that there was a master criminal stalking the streets, and they were united in their determination to capture this villain. I went past a brick house surrounded by a fence, and suddenly a large dog appeared. It came at me growling, baring its sharp, white teeth. The watchmen were still after me blowing their whistles, but now they were being joined by an ever-increasing number of local dogs. I finally made it to the fields next to the town. The freshly ploughed ground was soft and muddy, and I sank in up to my ankles at every step. The dogs were still after me, as were the watchmen. I ran. I ran away into the night. I noticed a yellow light in the distance; the station's lamp. I started heading towards it. The dogs were only a few steps behind me. Then I found myself crossing a graveyard. It sent shivers down my spine. I ran through the terrible graveyard, full of gravestones. Some leaning, some straight, some fallen over. I was gripped by terror, sweating profusely...

I suddenly remembered a rhyme, a little spell taught to

me as a child. I said it twenty, perhaps fifty times over, shouting it at the dogs:

"Be silent, be still, and lose all your will!"

When we were young children, that was our special spell against dogs. I'd learnt it off by heart as a child, in the belief that it would stop dogs in their tracks and bind their mouths. The dogs paid no attention to it whatsoever. So, having lost all hope of escaping them, I curled up into a ball on the ground, holding my head between my hands. I stayed like that for some time. I then tried to run again, but to no avail. I was knee deep in mud. Pulling up one foot left the shoe behind, so I had to wrestle my shoes out by hand. Then lightning started to flash, illuminating the dark clouds. A bitterly cold wind sprang up, bringing with it pouring rain with huge, splattering droplets. I was drenched within seconds. A short time later the wind picked up and carried the clouds away with it. The moon appeared. There were newly formed puddles everywhere, reflecting the silvery moonlight. Bright, sparkling puddles...

The dogs had long since run off, and I hadn't even noticed. I had gone a long way, and was finally out of the graveyard. A little while later I came to a road and quickened my pace, heading once again towards the station. The yellow light was coming from a wooden hut in front of the station. I walked right up to it, and looked in through the window.

Ahh, people!

The two guards were playing backgammon. I was so delighted to see a human face, I started humming a little tune. I felt like barging in and hugging them!

I went into the station.

Morning came. The sun was shining brightly, and it was a sparkling, wet, but warm and sunny day, typical for the South. The train was exactly six hours late. In spite of the warm sun, I was shivering from head to toe. My teeth were chattering. I bought my ticket from the counter, turned around, and came face to face with my grandfather's friend.

I dropped my ticket.

But...

"Goodness me, boy," he said, "look at the state you're in! Fell over in the mud? Got caught in the rain? What time did you leave in the morning anyway? The wife is awfully worried. If we'd have known you were leaving that early, she could have left some breakfast out for you last night! Ah, you have your ticket. Just a minute, let me get mine."

I was stunned.

"Come on then. We can talk on the train. I had some business that came up suddenly..."

"You must enter the high school exams," he said, once we had settled into the compartment. "Get that piece of paper. You don't know what might happen. I think you should go into higher education as well. Because your father..."

I was so delighted, I could barely contain myself.

"Well, that's what I plan to do. Not just university, but the European exams too..."

"Good on you. That should be your goal. You have to consider the family you come from..."

When I got home my mother gave me dry clothes, made me a hot herbal tea, and put a hot water bottle down my back.

"So," she asked, "did you manage to get anything out of him? Did you see Abdulfettah?"

Oh, no! My God! I had forgotten completely... That's why I had gone in the first place!

"I saw him," I lied, "but it was no use... 'If you think you have rights, I'll see you in court,' he said."

The hopeful look in my mother's eyes faded. My sisters lowered their heads. Our youngest turned to one of her sisters.

"Hasn't he brought back any money, then?" she

whispered.

She was only six.

XIII

I went back to the fields, back to thinking of God, and of his mysterious ways.

Bad things came from God, and good things came from God. A good fate was God's doing, and so was a bad one. God could be generous, but He could also be miserly. God made you laugh, He also made you cry. God created, God destroyed, and God let the devil have his way. And it was us, His servants, on the receiving end of it all!

My brain was addled with these mystifying dichotomies. I was only twenty, and my only sin was that I was the son of that exiled man.

And so the days went by.

One Sunday morning, our gang of three – Gazi, Hasan Hussein and I – met up at the café in the commercial quarter, near that cloth factory we had worked in.

It was one of those days for reminiscing. The weavers, Ahmet and Reshat came and joined us too.

"Are you in for a game, Hasan Hussein?" asked Gazi.

Hasan Hussein was wiping his glass eye with his handkerchief.

"Of?"

"Backgammon, Gulbahar rules."

"Sure. What're we playing for?"

"A packet of Serkidoryan."

"I'm in. Let's see your money."

They both gave me their money. The loser would put a fresh packet of cigarettes on the table, and we would get to smoke them until they were all gone.

They sat down facing each other. Ahmet, Reshat, I, and the others we knew from work crowded around. I noticed a worker at one of the nearby tables, wearing blue overalls, dark glasses, and reading a newspaper.

"Who's that man?" I asked Ahmet. "Does he work in

your factory?"

"He does," he replied, "How did you know?"

"You remember when that shuttle flew off while we were there... He stood up to the factory owner. Isn't that him?"

"Yes, that's him alright... Master Izzet, they call him. He's worked in all sorts of places. A very skilled man. He has this wife, a Bosnian woman, she's very sound too. Not sure what he is, they say he's Kurd."

Gazi and Hasan Hussein were making so much noise that Master Izzet had to put his paper down, and turn his chair to watch their game. Just at that point Gazi threw a double-one and went wild. He felt certain that he would now win with a backgammon.

He stood up, and offered everyone cigarettes in celebration of his decisive double-one. Hasan Hussein was cursing his luck.

Gazi played the double-one, then the double-two, then, as he was playing the double-three, Master Izzet spoke up.

"Not there, son," he said, "You don't want to do that... Bad move!"

Gazi took back his third three.

"Why's that?"

"Think of how the moves will go. You're not going to be able to come out after the third five on the double-five, and you'll ruin the backgammon!"

Master Izzet then took out his tin of tobacco, started rolling himself a cigarette, and lost all further interest in the game.

Gazi hesitated for a long time.

"Double-three three," he finally moved, "and double-three four. Now to the double-four. Double-four one, double-four two, and the other two: four! Hah! That was one four for our Hasan here, one four for my future kids, one four for..."

Hasan Hussein didn't take the ribbing well.

"Yeah, OK. Very good. So you've played your double

four. Get on with it!"

The people around found it all rather entertaining. Hasan Hussein's red-striped college of commerce cap had slipped to one side. He swore at Gazi.

"Hey, watch your mouth!" said Gazi, "Mind your manners..."

"I'll leave the bloody game. If you want to play, play properly!"

"You can leave any time you want. The money's safe... Was that meant to be a threat? Ok, then... Now, the double-five. Double-five one, that's the second, here's the third... Double-five three, double-five three, hey, Hasan, how many fives was that? Hmm? Was that the thi,rd? Go on Hasan, tell me. That was three fives so far, wasn't it?"

Master Izzet was still busy rolling his cigarette.

Having played his third five, Gazi was stuck. Hasan turned his good eye towards the café's service door.

"Excuse me," he called out, "could we have a fourth five for the gentleman here, please?"

Gazi turned to Master Izzet.

"Why did you interfere just then?" he asked angrily. "It wasn't any of your business, was it? What did you think you were doing?"

"You are so right," said the man, "I do apologise. I shouldn't have said anything."

He lit his cigarettes, and offered us tobacco. But Gazi was still angry. He slammed the backgammon board shut, and left.

After that Sunday I started going to that café regularly and slowly became friends with this Master Izzet, who had first caught my attention all that time ago.

One day, having listened to me rant anarchically for some time, he stopped me mid-sentence.

"So what?" he asked.

Hadn't he been listening to all the things I'd been telling him? The injustice, the inequality, God, the Devil, people, this, that, the other...

"What you're saying," he continued, "is that everyone on earth, and the Almighty above, have all stopped everything they were doing, just to give you a bad time."

"Are you taking the mickey?"

"Certainly not. I don't take the mickey out of people. But you have been painting such a picture, that this is the impression you've left me with. I hope I'm mistaken, because I would hate to think that anyone could be quite such an egotist."

"What's an egotist?"

"Someone who's selfish."

"Selfish?"

"Someone who considers himself to be the centre of the universe, and feels that the universe ought to arrange itself accordingly."

"Am I like that?"

"I hope you can free yourself of that attitude."

"So I am..."

"I genuinely hope you can free yourself from it."

This was a slap in the face for me. Should I run away in shame, or turn on the man for a fight?

But he left me no time to decide.

"I know of your father and his political escapades," he said, "and you've been filling in the gaps for me during these past few days. You are certainly suffering and, I suppose, like any sufferer you are entitled to your rebellious feelings. But I would strongly advise you not to come here, in the midst of those who have a far better case for rebelling, and wallow in self-pity while talking emptily of rebellion!"

I was completely under his spell, and I felt crushed. I felt I should say something.

"We all have our problems," he continued, "There's no such thing as a problem-free life. Particularly in this quarter, here. People living around here have huge problems. Food is a problem. Fuel is a problem. Sleep is a problem. Tuberculosis is a problem. Malaria is a problem.

And God knows what else... Let me phrase this in your words: This is the neighbourhood that God forgot. There are many here who have far better reasons for being angry than you do."

He re-lit his cigarette, and lost interest in me.

That day went by, as did others. We still talked, but now only about inconsequential things. In fact, he didn't seem that keen on talking to me at all. About ten days after his lecture, he suddenly pulled me up.

"Why don't you get yourself a job?"

I asked him who would dare to allow the son of an exiled man to work in their office.

"Ah," he said, "so you're a millionaire, then?"

"No..."

"Well, if you're not, then you must have relatives who look after you."

"Our relatives don't help..."

"There's no reason why they should."

"There isn't?"

"Of course not. Did they share your father's ideals?"

"No..."

"Well, then... So?"

"To be honest with you, I have no idea where our money comes from. I don't know who does what."

"So, you have no idea where the money comes from? Have you never felt curious? Never seen the need to find out?"

"Well, things are so tight..."

"All the more reason for you to find out how you do get by. Have you never thought to ask 'Mother, where does our money come from?' Have you never wondered?"

"You have a very odd way of talking..."

"Is that so?"

That day went by too. The following day, I was still annoyed. I did not go back to the café. I wandered on my own, thinking, calculating, wondering. The day after that, in spite of everything, I went back. He was there, reading his paper. We exchanged pleasantries, he put his paper away, and asked me where I had been yesterday.

"Nowhere," I said, "I had something to do."

"And what was that? Don't tell me you applied for a job?"

"No... As I've been telling you, I don't even have a middle-school diploma, and I'm the son of an exile..."

"I was saying 'get a job'. You're the one who took it to mean ' go and work in an office'."

"What else could I do?"

"Office workers aren't the only people on earth. They aren't even major contributors. Furthermore, the majority of the people on earth don't have middle-school diplomas. Yet they all work, earn, live, struggle, and enable those with diplomas to live, too!"

I had not grasped what he was saying.

"Is that not so?" he asked.

"Yes..."

"Well, then... Now let me give you a couple of pieces of advice: Firstly, think about all the different work that people can do, and get yourself a job. Secondly, get yourself used to listening, and allowing others to talk! You washed dishes in Beirut, you could do that here too. Or, I don't know, you could go and sell yoghurt."

I laughed.

"Why do you laugh? This is a perfectly serious matter."

"If we were in another town maybe I could, but..."

"But you can't here. Wouldn't want to be seen doing it, hmm? 'What would people say?' They'll think, 'He was such a great man, and now look at his son!' won't they? They'll all look down on you..."

"...?"

"You value yourself too highly. You think that people have nothing better to do but to concern themselves with you. That's an illness. It's the illness of those who have to get off a horse and mount a donkey, or, more accurately, fail to find a donkey and end up having to walk. You must fight this disease, or it will destroy you. All this moaning and complaining, it doesn't do any good at all. It will shut you away in your own mind. You will become a prisoner, trapped in your own mind. You have got to overcome this. Furthermore... But you must also wonder why I'm taking the time to talk to you like this. Maybe you think me strange. But I can see that you're a bright young man. You have got to shake this thing off. Mankind needs bright young minds. That's why I'm putting in an effort."

We no longer met at the café. We now arranged to meet in the fields, and walk around in open air.

"You must rid yourself of your awful self-pity. It will imprison you in your own mind. You will become your own worst enemy. It will ruin you!"

"But what should I do?"

"You should beat that feeling. Try it. First, get yourself a job. Any job. Somewhere out of town, maybe. Digging dirt, something like that. You may find it's too much, but stick with it. Try to manage. There's nothing one can't manage, if one sets one's mind to the task. If others can manage something, and you can't, it'll be your attitude. It's that attitude you have to beat. Then, as time goes on, you can work your way in towards the centre of town. Then one day, you'll realise that no one's paying you a blind bit of notice, and you will have brought down the walls of your prison for good!"

I then told him the story of the former Member of the High Court, and how I had run away in the middle of the night and been chased by dogs. He burst out laughing.

"You did get carried away, didn't you?"

"Well... Don't you think I'm ugly, though?"

"Not particularly."

"My hooked nose? Withered hands?"

"They're hardly..."

He paused, and continued solemnly.

"Many people are aware of their own faults," he said,

"but most people would try and hide them. Knowing your own faults is one admirable quality, and the ability to talk about them is another. Particularly if you can be objective about your attitude. Well done. That's very good."

"Are you saying I'm not so ugly I would scare people away?"

"Certainly not. And you have a perfectly good colour. You have nothing to worry about! But all that aside, you really must find yourself a job, OK?"

Three days later I found myself a gravel shovelling job at a building site, three-quarters-of-an-hour's drive away from town. At five o'clock the next morning I went and stood in front of the radiator of a large, double rear-axle Dodge truck with twenty-two other dishevelled workmen. We clambered up onto the back, clutching our picks and shovels. I stood among these tanned, rough-looking strangers, and lit a cigarette as the truck tore through the icy early morning air. The truck really did seem to be flying along. I stood straight and firm, my shovel resting on my shoulder, taking a perverse pleasure in blowing my cigarette smoke towards the still slumbering farmhouses and mansions we passed.

One of the workers was singing a central-Anatolian folk song.

I was so excited! It was like the time Gazi and I first went to work at the factory. I wanted to shout out, to swear at all those farmhouses and mansions, to announce to the world that I was off to earn my own living now, I wanted everyone to know. I wanted to say: Take your diploma, and shove it!

I wasn't thinking of my hooked nose, my withered fingers, my holed shoes or my frayed trousers. My workmates paid no attention to me. They all had their lunch-bags, and most of them were smoking...

Suddenly our truck rounded a sharp bend, and we found ourselves facing a steep precipice ahead of us. When the truck rounded the next sharp bend, the precipice suddenly moved to our left. It was a terrible, steep drop. Meanwhile the sun had started to rise, a red ball behind a fluffy pink veil. Mother nature was rubbing her eyes and slowly waking up.

Our truck finally arrived at the site and we jumped off. Everyone apart from me, all these brown, sun-baked, rugged men, were all familiar with the work. They all gripped their picks and shovels purposefully. The foreman blew his whistle, and we attacked the gravel. Some of us dug, and some of us shovelled it onto the truck. I was shovelling. I had made a good, energetic start... I was now earning my bread with my own sweat, and I was going to deserve what I earned.

The workmate next to me, shovelling alongside me, noticed my enthusiasm.

"Gently, mate, gently," he said, "you want to ease up a little."

But I was off.

My burst of energy didn't last long. I had started to feel a pain gripping my shoulders. The truck seemed to take forever to fill, and the pain grew stronger. As the pain took hold of me, I found it more and more difficult to breathe. Then, my ribs started to hurt...

Finally, the truck was full. We would have a breather until it emptied its load and came back. I sat down under a rock, next to the young lad I had been shovelling with.

"What's your name then?" he asked, unenthusiastically.

I told him.

"And yours?"

"Mine? I'm 'Sugar' Veli."

"Where are you from?"

"Me? I'm from Yildizeli. And you?"

"Oh, I'm local."

"Yeah, I'm from Yildizeli... I came here last year, and the year before... I used to go to Ankara... Is this your first time doing this?

"It is."

"This is a tough job, mate. Don't reckon you'll be able to hack it. Couldn't you wangle a desk job or something?"

"I couldn't, mate. So, you don't think I'll hack it. How comes you manage, then?"

"You don't want to go by what I can do. I've always done the heavy stuff, me. Brought up that way... My dad did this work, and his dad before him."

"How do you know I haven't done heavy work?"

"Look at your hands, mate. Those are clerking hands. And you're face is white. That's not seen any sun, has it? And what are you going to eat for lunch? You've no bread or anything. There's no restaurants around here, you know!"

He smelled of sweat.

"Not to worry, mate," he continued, "we'll share my food."

It wasn't long before the truck came back. My arms, my shoulders and my chest were all in pain, as if I was wounded. And on the third return of the truck, my arms stopped working. It was as if someone had severed all the nerves. I felt sick inside, cold and clammy all over, and totally out of energy. No matter what I did, I was unable to move my arms. I stopped.

"Told you, didn't I?" said Sugar Veli, "You really shouldn't be here, mate. Can't be running out of steam now..."

Then the foreman came. He'd smell out anyone being idle, and go up and start having a go, and throw stones at them. He spotted me, shouted and yelled, and threw a huge stone straight at me.

"What are you stopping for, eh? What are you stopping for? We're paying you to do a day's work here!"

I tried to move, but to no avail. So the foreman swore at me, long and dirty. I immediately swore back, and threw down my spade. Everyone laughed. The foreman came over.

"Finding it difficult, are we?" he said, "Why didn't you just stay in daddy's mansion? Think you were coming on a picnic, did you?"

"I'm not doing this!" I said.

"You what?"

"I said, I'm not doing it!"

"Couldn't hack it, could you? Thought it would be like working for your daddy, eh? 'I'm not doing this'! Well, you're not hungry, are you? 'Not doing this'!"

Although I knew it was not a brave act, I set off towards town on foot.

This manual labouring was even harder than weaving on the looms. I realised that the people who did this sort of work weren't built like me at all. They were made of iron or steel, or something.

XIV

"I didn't expect anything else," said my friend in the blue-overalls. "You went and chose the heaviest work possible. No matter… As for what the foreman said… Now, that doesn't seem to have bothered you at all. I wonder why? He made some quite cutting remarks, didn't he?"

That was true… I suddenly realised that I hadn't been bothered by it.

"Because," he said, "in spite of everything, you still believe yourself to be his better. The people who annoy you are those of your own class, aren't they? Those you can't bring yourself to accept as your betters. Hmm?

Then, one day, the man in the blue overalls disappeared. Where had he come from anyway? Who was he? What was he up to?

I never knew. But he had had quite an effect on me.

"You have to get used to not getting angry," he had told me, "People don't want anger, they want sympathy, and love. Try to be like a doctor, never getting angry with your patients. Earn a living with an honest day's work; buy plenty of books, read a lot… You don't need to know who I am. I'm just another human being…"

A while later my mother and my sisters somehow managed to collect up enough for their fares, and they left me in the care of God first, my grandmother second, and set off one evening to return to my father's side.

XV

I eventually ended up back at the old factory. You know; the one where Gazi and I had woven cloth on the machines… But this time, as an accounts clerk!

My monthly salary was exactly twenty-four liras and ninety-five kurus, and I had no doubt in my mind that this gave me complete freedom, and the ability to travel, open my factory, even start my own bank!

Most of the guys in our department were experts at choosing clothes and ties, separating the girls from the women. They all had greased back hair and carefree laughs. Still, their hearts were in the right place. They wanted to get the most out of life, to live life to the full, be it in a bar, a tavern, or a brothel. Books were useful only if they contained explicit sexual scenes, or as aids to chatting up girls. Although they would bow their heads and take the most insulting of remarks from the factory owner, the managing director, or the chief accountant, they would behave like titans when faced with a bar girl, or a waiter.

My line-manager was a man about my age who had also left middle school in its final year. He was as highly-strung as a taut steel wire.

"I will learn it all," he would say, "and one day, make it to the top!"

His obsession for learning used to get on the nerves of everyone in the department. No bars, taverns or brothels for him! He had no desire to dress well, or to get himself a lover. He just wanted to learn things, whether they were relevant to him or not.

"I was only about this tall when my father died," he

would say, "And my mother had to go out and do laundry. I had to walk the streets selling milk, selling yoghurt, selling pasties, selling papers, shining shoes… But I was studying at the same time. I would have studied more, except for my mother's illness. Whatever it is that's wrong with her, I'm going to find out all about it. Why shouldn't one person be able to learn what another can? After all, professors are people too, just like you and me."

He would solve the most complicated algebraic equations with ease, and took it on himself to know all the calculations and figures from every department of the factory: Electricity, expenditure, thread, the yield of the machinery and even the settings on individual machines, absolutely everything!

Although he desperately tried to conceal it, I had seen him spit blood. He wanted to rise, to be on a good income. His ultimate aim was to migrate to Switzerland. I asked him once why Switzerland – as opposed to, say, France, Italy, England or America?

"Because," he explained, "I consider Switzerland to be the most civilised country in the world. Moreover, they make the best watches in the world."

The day I saw him spit blood, I knew why he wanted to go to Switzerland. But everything aside, I did admire his desire to "learn". He knew I was an avid reader, but wondered what I wanted to do with my life.

I couldn't very well turn around to him and say, "My ambition is to become a person who says nice things to people!"

"Don't waste your time," he would always advise me, "Set your sights high, and study to get there!" And he would immediately add:

It takes no skill to be born, so now
You must raise yourself up in the world.

One of my friends in the accounts department was a guy called Himmet, the son of a lawyer. He was short, skinny and put me in mind of a dried-out carrot. He'd drink wine on an empty stomach with the aim of gaining weight, and shave his whole head all year round, just to look different. He was my age. He had lost his father while he was still at primary school. He had only been able to continue his schooling until the second year of middle school, and then he had to go and earn a living.

"My father was a lawyer," he'd say, "I can't stay a two-bit clerk all my life. No-one seems to be willing to take me on, though, so I'm going to have to find ways to make people take notice of me!"

He would add that he knew just how to do that.

"When I have a drink, I'm really great. I start talking fluently. No hesitation, no holding back. Everyone stops and listens to me. Let me give you a word of advice: Don't let other people get a word in! You've got to be talking non-stop."

"And then?"

"I can tell you that based on my experience, people give in to you! You tell them all sorts of things, use all the words you know, and they might not understand everything you've said but, believe me, they remember who you are after that! The thing is, eighty percent of people don't think about what's being said, but they remember who spoke, and how things were said."

He worked at the spare parts section at the factory and, like me, he was on twenty-four liras and ninety-five kurus a month, but he knew the amounts of each and every one of the two-thousand odd items in stock. He could tell you off the top of his head how many had come in, how many had gone out, and how many he had in stock.

He would arrive each morning with a speech for me, drag me to one side of the warehouse, and start talking to me among the smells of engine oil and machine belts. He would conclude the speech with gusto, and as he wiped the sweat off his brow, he would ask my opinion.

"How was that for a speech?"

If I liked it, he'd buy me a tea. If I hadn't:

"You," he would say, "are not yet in a position to really understand all that."

If I stuck to my guns he would get angry, and ask me the meaning of one of the long words, which he tended to insert into his speech at various points. I knew full well that he saw these words in his father's old reference books, looked up their meanings in dictionaries, learnt them off by heart, and questioned me about them later, purely to establish the superiority of his knowledge.

So I usually approved his speeches, and told him that "I couldn't imagine a better speech," just so that I didn't have to sit through his tedious explanations. Then he'd be delighted, and congratulate me for my insight.

"I can see you're coming along tremendously!" he'd say.

I had now got a taste for getting others to talk while I listened. This development had made me lots of friends, and I found myself being very popular.

I made friends with some of the other guys in accounts too. Especially with Turhan and Mustafa.

Those two sat at the same desk, doing the same job. They were very close friends but, at the same time, they would sometimes be at each other's throats too. Turhan had left high school in his final year, and was the son of a bankrupt trader. He was withered and skinny, and had a very crooked nose. However he had this thing about how good-looking he was. His drawer was full of eau de cologne, brilliantine and liquid Vaseline. He'd forever be holding his mirror, freshening himself up and plucking his eyebrows with a pair of tweezers. He would carefully scan those around him and if he felt he had been seen preening he would get cross, argue, and not talk to people.

Mustafa was completely different. Quite the opposite of Turhan he was relaxed, and would jest, laugh, and was generally much more fun to be with. He had only managed to finish primary school. He would follow Turhan around being his yes-man, always approving his words or actions. One day, I asked him why he did this.

"I have to be close to him," he explained, "You see, the women he fancies always end up liking me better!"

In fact, their whole friendship revolved around being at bars, and the women they picked up at bars.

They both loved the same woman. Or rather, Turhan was smitten with the woman, and the woman fancied Mustafa. Now Mustafa was genuinely good looking. In fact Turhan was only really trying to emulate him, but he couldn't bear the thought of anyone noticing this.

One day he got very angry at Mustafa, again for no apparent reason. He went almost purple with rage. Right at that moment, Mustafa whipped out his pocket mirror.

"Look at that! See how awful you look?" he said, suddenly holding it to Turhan's face.

Turhan went mad. He threw everything on his desk around the office; books, pencils, the inkwell, the blotter, they all went flying. He swore and cursed... And just before he stormed out of the accounts office, his whole body in a knot of rage, he stopped and turned around.

"You bastard," he said, "one of these days I'm going to kill you. You see if I don't!"

Mustafa was laughing at him. He sobered up once Turhan had left.

"That wasn't nice, was it? Do you think I should go after him, and try and make up?"

"What on earth for?"

"Because... Well, he is very ugly, and he knows it. It gets to him."

I went and found Turhan in the thread warehouse. He was sitting between a couple of boxes, crying silently to himself. When he heard my footsteps he suddenly straightened up, and started rubbing his eyes.

"I'm glad you've come. I seem to have got something in my eyes... Could you take a look?"

I inspected his eyes, gently blew on them, and went along with the theory that he must have had something in them.

Turhan didn't speak to Mustafa for a long time after that. He frequently called me to his table.

"You know," he would say to me, "It's actually rather upsetting to have to work next to all these uneducated, ignorant people. I do hope I pass my exams and get into university."

As he said this sort of thing he would be surreptitiously keeping an eye on Mustafa, and he'd get annoyed if Mustafa wasn't paying attention.

"He's ignorant!" he'd say, "The worthless sod."

On one occasion Mustafa had called out to a friend of his across the room.

"Guess what?" he'd said, "I'm going to Hollywood soon!"

"To Hollywood? Really?"

"Yeah, really! I've had an offer from Metro-Goldwyn-Meyer, and I'm going to be an actor. It seems they were after a new leading man…"

Turhan immediately turned purple, threw away his pencil, and stormed out.

Mustafa had burst out laughing.

"Look here," Turhan said to me, when the two of them had finally made up, "today we're off to the bar to drink to your health, so you've got to come along."

"Me?" I said, "I've never been to a bar in my life… I don't know how to dance, either."

"No problem. You can just have a beer, and eye up the birds. I'll introduce you to my one. You wait till you see her… Now she is something!"

At the end of work that day, the three of us left together.

It was genuinely the first time I'd ever been to a bar. I felt overwhelmed by the loud band, the cigarette smoke, the smell of alcohol, the multi-coloured clothes and the women. I suddenly thought of my own appearance, my clothes and my nose. I didn't feel as bad as I once might have, but I still felt rather awkward and out of place.

We ordered the beers. There was this flurry of activity which had nothing to do with us, something of a panic in the barkeeper's eyes, and a preoccupied bustle on the part of the waiters. A few tables were pulled over and set up next to the dance floor. The waiters quickly got the tables ready. Knives, forks and plates clattered, waiters weaved their way through the crowd, and the owner of the bar, elegant in his tuxedo but looking young enough to be in his teens, nervously hovered around the tables, anxiously checking on his staff. Once he was satisfied that the tables were in order, he turned to the band.

"Let's have something to dance to!"

The band played, and he whirled to the centre of the dance floor, to the enthusiastic applause of the bar girls.

"I guess the heavyweights are coming!"

"Who are the heavyweights?" I asked.

"You'll see."

A moment later, the outside double doors of the bar swung wide open. A group of large, powerful-looking men sauntered in. The crowed parted for them, and everyone – led by the bar owner and his staff – stood in awe. The bar girls all stood up.

"See the VIP's?" said Mustafa.

These were wealthy men, and they were here to spend. The three in front were visibly tired and drawn, in spite of their imposing girths. They all pulled up their chairs and sat down at the tables. The women were called over, and the bar was opened up to them. And I mean opened up: Raki, beer, wine, vermouth, champagne, gin, it was all flowing. They paid no attention to the people around.

"They are spending big time!" grumbled Turhan, "Big time!"

"Tell me," said Mustafa, "What university could hope to award a diploma that would give you all that?"

"I bet they wouldn't know where the Cape of Good Hope is, though…"

"Don't have to go that far, mate. You'd only have to ask them what eight times nine is."

I said nothing. But... Could it be fate, giving them all that?

Then I suddenly remembered my friend in the blue overalls, and his words that this sort of thinking would do me no good, and only make me miserable.

By midnight, the rich men's drunkenness had reached crazy levels. The women were being crudely groped, wetly kissed, roughly fondled and squeezed. Eventually they decided that they'd had enough of it all, and asked for their bill. What bill? They didn't even glance at the paper put down by the headwaiter, who had been keeping careful notes of everything going to their table throughout the evening. Large hands sporting numerous gold rings dove into wallets, and those wallets opened to reveal huge wads of notes. The men peeled off five-hundred lira notes. They threw the notes towards the owner of the bar. The bar owner didn't know what to do. None of the men wanted the others to be paying, but they eventually sorted it out. The bar owner, magnificent though his tuxedo was, crawled all over the floor on his hands and knees, picking up the five-hundred lira notes as if they had been holy scriptures. He then carefully arranged their change on a sparklingly clean white plate, and presented this to them. But none of the men would touch the change and, leaving that small fortune by way of a tip, they got up to leave. Everyone in the bar applauded them.

The band started a foxtrot. The bar, as if suddenly remembering what it was all about, and that it had in fact been a bar all along, suddenly sprang back to life.

A little later the joint lover of Turhan and Mustafa came over to our table, adjusting her bra along the way. She stroked Turhan's jaw, and winked at Mustafa. Turhan, unaware of the wink, looked at me with pride, clearly pleased with himself, like a man who knows he is loved.

The woman pulled up a chair and sat down. She started

to freshen up her makeup.

"You're not cross with me, are you?" she asked Turhan.

Turhan was delighted. He immediately leaned over towards me.

"Did you hear that?" he asked, "She's asking me if I'm cross with her! I told you... She's knows to show respect."

When Turhan went to the toilet a short while later, Mustafa leant over.

"What did he tell you? That she showed respect? You just wait a while; you'll see what happens..."

And so I did. Turhan got so drunk... He first rested his head on the table, then he swayed back and forth on his chair, then he started to collapse. He ended up on the concrete floor of the bar. He lay on his back on the concrete, laughing out loud, describing huge circles in the air with a shaky finger, and shouting out the name of the woman in pink.

The woman was already tête-à-tête with Mustafa. I went to lift Turhan up.

"Oh, please don't trouble yourself;" she said to me, "He's the happiest man in the world, like this. Especially when I give him one of my shoes."

With that, she carefully took off one of her small, dainty pink shoes, and dropped it over towards Turhan. Turhan took it, rubbed his face and mouth all over it, and started kissing it.

Should I feel sorry for a man like that, or should I feel disgusted?

The woman in pink adjourned to one of the rooms with Mustafa. Turhan was still lying on the floor, stretching out towards the shoe that had just been taken away from him and shouting out the woman's name. A waiter marched over, holding a long broom.

"Get up!" he said, kicking Turhan, "Get out, you disgusting bastard!"

I'm not sure exactly why, but I leapt up and shoved the

waiter away. I was drunk too, and I suppose it hadn't occurred to me that the waiter might have a point. I don't remember quite what I said to him, nor what he said in reply.

But I do remember him eventually saying, "Look mate, I'm only human. I know this is my job and everything, but there are limits! I'm sick and tired of this guy. You would be too. He's like this every bloody night. And here I am, leaving my pregnant wife alone at home all through the night, just to earn a crust. It's not right!"

His eyebrows stretched his wrinkled face upwards, and I noticed the glint of tears on his eyelashes.

Mustafa had sent word, so I went over to the room he was in. The woman in pink was there sitting on Mustafa's lap, breastfeeding a little baby. I went to get back out.

"Come in, come in!" said Mustafa, "I'm not a jealous man like Turhan is! You can have my lady lover too, if you want!"

My stomach turned, the walls swayed, the floors moved around, and the ceiling started to spin. I mumbled something about there being no need for that much generosity.

The woman in pink called out, "Mother!"

A small, dark woman, headscarf tied tightly under her chin, hesitantly came through the doorway to the side of the room. The woman in pink passed the baby over. She was still on Mustafa's lap, and obviously saw no reason to get down. The mother, embarrassed not just on her own account but for her daughter as well, took the child and silently withdrew.

"God, I must have drunk a lot yesterday!" said Turhan the following day. "Still, it was a laugh, eh?"

"...?"

"So, what did you think of my woman, then? Do you like her?"

"Yes, she seems very nice..."

"She's lovely. She is so considerate, so willing to

please. She'd do anything for me, you know..."

"...?"

"You what she likes best about me? The colour of my eyes. They're a lovely, delicate hazel, she tells me."

The only thing that really played on my mind, though, wasn't Turhan's hazel eyes, nor the woman in pink, nor Mustafa. It was that shy, wizened woman, who had reminded me of my own mother. I felt awful whenever I thought of her.

I found out from Mustafa that that little old lady had been a teacher, and was still getting a pension from her career.

XVI

Himmet listened to all this angrily.

"It's a disgrace," he declared, "an absolute disgrace! A whole generation is being lost to decadence."

I asked him why he said that.

He gave me a harsh stare. He then launched into a history lesson, starting with our valiant ancestors from Central Asia, tracing our glorious path through history, and really got carried away as he went on with the lecture, barely pausing to breathe. Once he got fully warmed to his subject he became quite animated, and started waving his arms in the air and punching invisible targets. Judging by the energy he spoke with, you would think he was addressing an audience of thousands.

We had made it all the way to the reasons behind the fall of the Ottoman Empire when the door opened gently, and the tall, large-nosed managing director appeared. Himmet's waving arm and punching fist froze in mid-air.

"Preaching again, Himmet Effendi?" asked the managing director, "Preaching again?"

"And you, sir?" he said, turning to me, "What are you doing here? How many times have I told you about this, hmm? How many times? Have I not told you that attending to private matters on company time is a form of stealing? Why does no one listen to what I tell them?"

"I was after the inventory records for the..."

"Be quiet! I've been listening from behind the door!
The fall of the Ottoman Sultanate is none of your
business. You worry about your own fall. Listen to me,
gentlemen. This is your final warning. Come on! You will
lose your livelihood, lads, so help me you will. You can
dream up all your theories, all your projects, and all the
scenarios you want, but not on our company time. We
want honest workers; not people who steal time while
others work. We don't want rulers, or party leaders, or
sociologists... Go on, the pair of you, get back to work!"

Well, in all fairness, the managing director did have a
point about standing around, giving lectures like that. As
for how much of it was my fault... Well, no one was
going to take my side anyway. But in terms of standing up
against the managing director, well... I did need that
twenty-four ninety-five at the end of the month.

XVII

Time passed, and Himmet left the company. Mustafa
and Turhan went off to do their military service, and my
chief – who had mumbled all that time about going to
Switzerland – passed away. And I, mostly because I
couldn't think of anything better to do, fell in love.

The paved road passing in front of the battleship-grey
factory gates split into three, its branches leading off into
the districts where workers lived. At six o'clock in the
evening these streets would fill with all the people
working in the commercial district: the girls from the
thread factories, the stackers, the labourers, the weavers,
and the plump old cleaning ladies...

Although our department was meant to work until
seven, I would almost always call it a day at around half
past five, and go over to the sour-smelling wine-cellar of
the co-operative across the road from the factory. I would
settle myself down by the street-level window of the wine-
cellar, fill up my large glass full of their ruby-red wine and

light a cigarette, and get myself ready to watch the bubbling crowd of girls leave the thread factory in half an hour's time.

I would knock back the first, second and third glasses without any mezes, and notice my vision blur as I became a slightly tipsy. This would have a light, sweet effect, and I'd forget all about my withered hands and hooked nose in the freedom it afforded me.

Where did half an hour go? Did I really knock back eight glasses just like that?

The girls came out, their black pinafores coated in cotton dust. All the girls who worked on the spinning wheels, the looms and the workbenches... Huddled in groups of two or three, sometimes five or more. As they went by in quick, nervous steps some of them would subtly glance over, nudge each other and giggle.

One of them – and it was always her I noticed – was a very pretty girl. Bosnian, about fourteen. She would always make a point of obviously looking at me, walking a few steps more, and then turning around to look again, smiling each time. She would walk on, stop and turn, smile, walk on, stop and turn, smile. Right up until she disappeared around the corner.

I had no idea how I managed to get out of the wine-cellar and stagger after her. I stumbled along the crooked streets between workers' houses, doing my best to avoid the piles of rusty cans and rotting wood. The girls, who were only a few steps in front of me, had huddled together in a tight pack.

My insides were churning around like a stormy sea!

My eyes were fixed on her white cotton shoes on her somewhat skinny legs. Her hips were only beginning to take form. We were going through narrow crooked streets, flanked by crumbling brick houses. In front of most doors sat masculine looking Kurd women, peeling onions, washing their children, or lighting braziers and releasing bitter-smells into their neighbourhood. Then we got to a neighbourhood full of decorated eaves, ornate window-sills, and women with handfuls of knitting, exchanging anecdotes across the street. This was the Cretans' quarter. I knew that behind those windows that opened onto the street there were plenty of Cretan girls, giggling, and making sure that passers-by heard their exchanges in broken Turkish. They always stared invitingly and were known to be very forward. Generous, even. But what a useless line of thought that was. Here I was, twenty-two years of age, my girlfriend was all of fourteen, I was drunk, and I loved only her.

A sensuous laugh poured out of an open window I passed. Without even having to turn my head, I noticed that behind the white curtain which had been inexpertly embroidered with pink, green and purple thread, two women were holding their heads together. They pulled back every time I turned to look, but as I walked on, I heard their voices, pitched so that I would only just hear them.

"Ooo, mister! Why don't you come here a minute? I've something to tell you!"

Then, I followed the girls into the poor Bosnians' quarter.

A pale, tall and lean weaver, his jacket hanging loosely off his shoulders, eyes drooping with a lack of sleep, glanced at me harshly over his dark, thick moustache as he swept by. In fact, he paused for a second, weighing me up. I was aware of him staring at me right up until he turned the corner, but I didn't allow myself to be distracted. After all, I was twenty-two, in love, and I was carrying a polished steel flick-knife in my pocket.

Meanwhile my beloved entered a courtyard on the left, through a pair of aging wooden doors which were so covered in dirt they looked a leaden-grey. Seeing no reason to hide my quest, I stopped dead in my tracks. There was a long, dusty road to my right, which connected the city to the vineyards. I leaned back against an old wall, ignoring the lizards that were darting in and out of it, and turned to face the door to the courtyard. I stood there for some time.

On the road to my right, all sorts of people were making their way to the vineyards. Pedestrians, cyclists... There was an occasional motorcycle, whizzing past like a bullet, and the odd aging Chevrolet, leaving everything behind in a cloud of dust. The sun was slowly setting behind the ash-coloured soap factory. Everywhere I looked I saw dust, sweat, and people in a hurry.

Suddenly, my beloved came out. She had different shoes on her freshly washed feet, and was wearing a honey-coloured dress. She was clutching her jackstones, and was accompanied by two friends.

The whole world dissolved away around us!

I was vaguely aware of the various thin, tall men in tatty outfits, the women in white headscarves, and of the young men staring at me suspiciously or aggressively, all coming in and out of the courtyard door. None of them mattered.

Then a little girl quietly snuck up to me, and glanced around furtively.

"Mister," she said, "My sister says, if he loves me, she says, please tell him not to wait, she says. I'm afraid, she says. My father could get back from the mosque any minute, she says, or my brother might get back, she says..."

"Are you really her sister?"

"No..."

"Then who are you?"

"Her neighbour..."

I left, but only as a demonstration of my love for her.

I was on the road to the vineyards. After about a hundred, a hundred and fifty steps or so, my brain finally took over. "So what if her father comes? Or her brother? What does it matter? I'm going to marry her, aren't I?"

So I went back.

The evening had now really set in. The last of the labourers were hurrying past me in quite a rush. The ashen, zinc-walled soap factory had disappeared in the darkness. I returned to the spot where I had been standing, leaned my back against the crumbling wall, and started to watch the courtyard door again.

These sorts of courtyards had row upon row of doors inside, each one leading to a working family's home. The doors to the courtyards themselves always remained open. This one's latch had rotted away, its iron bolts were rusty, and the wood itself had weathered so much that it was no longer straight or even.

When it became completely dark, lights started to come on behind the white curtains in the windows. A man wandered down the street, coughing heavily. Occasionally a door opened gently, and then closed again. A child cried nearby. As darkness descended, the whole neighbourhood slowed to a halt. The only signs of life in the building were the dim yellow shafts of light, escaping from its many windows.

I could no longer see the courtyard door. I went to the street behind the building. My beloved's window would be looking out here. There was a sickening stench to the street, but I spotted the shadow of my beloved, flickering up and down behind her curtain as she played jackstones. I became completely focussed on her shadow, thinking all sorts of wild thoughts in that drunken state! For instance, I could walk on up to their door. Saunter into their home with a 'How do you do'. I could do; I certainly had no qualms about it. I'd like to see that tall, terse father of hers try and say anything. It seemed to me at that moment that I could conquer the earth, and I would certainly not hesitate to get blood on my hands and end the life of anyone who stood in my way. But I would never actually go through with anything like that. That type of thought would only ever exist in my imagination, mainly because I felt sorry for the girl, and would never want her to end up being at the centre of such a scandal.

Then, I saw her standing behind the curtain again. I dismissed all my thoughts with a shrug, and focussed back on the window, and stayed frozen like that for a number of minutes. Suddenly, I heard the heavy footsteps and whistle of a night watchman. I did not flinch. I didn't have the slightest concern about watchmen coming up to me, and asking me my business, suspecting I may be a thief.

Hours went by.

The silvery disc of the moon quietly emerged from behind a roof. The filthy street lit up in its ice-cold light. Later, having followed its path through the sky, the moon sank away, leaving me in darkness once again. Dawn was approaching. Still drunk and now very tired, I made my way back to my grandmother's bedsit.

She was such a light sleeper that even a passing cat would wake her. I did my best to tiptoe in quietly, so as not to wake her and get an earful. But I couldn't stop the slight crack from the door's hinges, nor the creaking of the floorboards. My grandmother was sitting bolt upright by the time I was through the door. She stared at me in the dim light of the bulb.

"Oh you wicked boy, you wicked boy! Have you any idea what I've been going through? I worried about you getting stabbed in some alley... I thought you might have got drunk and collapsed somewhere... I've been worried sick!"

I was in no mood to reply. I felt the need to whistle a merry tune as I thought about my beloved, her plaits flicking up and down as she moved behind her curtain, playing her game of jackstones.

"Not only does he tell me he has no money," said my grandmother, "and complains about how little he earns, he goes out every night drinking himself stupid! How do you get the raki if you have no money? Tell me that!"

She thinks that the only way to get drunk is by drinking raki, and that you have to pay up front for every drink you have. There is obviously no way to explain to the woman how these things work. It seems to me that she is simply not going to appreciate that I can get drunk without paying any money out first, nor is she going to understand that I'm in love with a factory girl. That sort of life is alien to her. Nor would she be willing to try and empathise. You see she is the mother of a "gentleman," and a mother-in-law to "gentlemen". The son and heir of a "gentleman" could not possibly "stoop so low" as to show interest in a "factory girl". If I were then to insist, she would give me strange looks, and her eyes would fill with tears.

"You," she would say, "are like your mother. Your mother was just like this. She used to love being all friendly with riff-raff!"

I don't remember how I got myself into bed, or how or when I fell asleep.

I woke up just after dawn, while the sky was still slightly pink. I was still drunk, and my head was still full of the two plaits of my beloved, bouncing as she played behind her curtain.

I got dressed. As I was leaving, my grandmother stopped me.

"Don't you have a few kurus?" she asked, "It's been such a long time since I last had a hot meal!"

But I knew she wasn't that dependent on me.

I was already at the street door. How would I have any money? If I had any, of course I'd give her some; I'm not that heartless! But my grandmother didn't know that the only thing payday was good for, was renewing my credit.

XVIII

It was evening time, and once again I was leaning against the lizard-infested wall, staring drunkenly at her courtyard door. A short, chubby, sweet-looking woman with a pock-marked face came up to me.

"Are you waiting for her?" she asked.

"Yes…" I said. My hand went to my shiny steel flick

knife resting in my pocket.

"What's that? Why have you put your hand in your pocket?"

"Er, nothing..."

"Now, now. You weren't going to pull a knife on a poor defenceless woman, were you?"

"Oh, no. I wasn't going for a knife..."

She moved in a little closer.

"Do you really love the girl, or are you just after a bit of fun?"

"I love her, I really do..."

"Do you? Really?"

"I swear to God!"

"The trouble is, there are others who love her too. I can't see them letting you have her... I think you may be wasting your time here."

"Who else loves her?"

"You're asking me who else loves her? Why, almost all of them! Look, this is a workers' district. They're all after a bright young girl like that!"

"But what if she didn't want them? Can't force happiness..."

"Well, I don't know that she is interested in anyone in particular. But her father, now, he has a temper on him... He wouldn't care who was interested in who, whether anyone carried a gun or a knife, or any of that business. Don't let him catch you here..."

"What would he do?"

"I don't know exactly what he would do, but all I'm saying is that it would be better if he didn't see you here. The girl also has an older brother who works in our factory, weaving cloth. Both these kids work, and once a fortnight they come and hand every penny they earn over to their father. The man was a very influential landowner back home... Everyone in the district feared him. Our fathers often told us of how he had sliced the heads off at least a few hundred infidels. So, don't judge him by where they live now... He's also capable of doing all sorts of work, but he won't. Thinks having a job is beneath him. You should see all the men who come and ask for his daughter's hand in marriage. Why only the other day the owner of the grocer's in Kurukopru was here, you know, the one just past Jumali's café. Now that man was crazy about the girl. Promising her a nice house, gold bracelets, diamond earrings, clothes... Who knows what else. What have you got? How can you top that? However you look at it, you're just a little clerk somewhere."

I was mortified.

"See? You've no answer to that, have you? A clerk in some factory. What would the two of you do? You'd have nothing between you. Being young doesn't put food on the table. I heard the man myself. 'If only she said yes,' he said, 'I would put the mansion in her name immediately,' he said. What about you? Have you talked to her? Does she like you?"

"No, we haven't talked."

"If you haven't even talked to her, why are you wandering around after her?"

"I don't know. I don't really know what I'm doing. I'm just following her... I can't help it."

"Give up, son, just give up. There are lots of men wandering around after this one. They'll corner you in some dark alley, and that'll be the end of you. Don't throw your life away like that. There are those offering your weight in gold for her... Honestly..."

Just then my "beloved", pretty in her honey-coloured dress, appeared at the courtyard door. She was looking at us from a distance. I moved away, all hopes dashed to pieces. I turned the corner in deep shame, and sped away.

Goodbye my desires, my sweet hopes, the moon above, rusty cans, rotting piles of wood, goodbye! Cats, dogs, brick-walled houses, Kurd women with masculine faces, crooked little streets and, last but not least, my little lovely with your prettily bouncing plaits behind your white curtain, goodbye!

And a curse on all the gold in the world!

I withdrew. I didn't go back to the wine-cellar, nor to the window I watched her from... Bitter, dark, boring days went by... One afternoon, I was gloomily sitting at my desk again. The caretaker came up to me. He told me there was a little girl waiting for me at the factory gates. I went to see. It was that little girl who had spoken to me all those days ago. She came up to me again, just like she had done that day.

"Mister," she said, "my sister said to tell you that her father is off to evening prayers tonight, and that her brother will be working. She says you should come around to the back window, and she's going to tell you something!"

"Who? Her? I don't... When? Really?"

"I swear!"

"When? Did you say the back window?"

"Yes. After evening prayers have started!"

I felt as if an inner wall crumbled, and I was being filled with sunlight. I wanted to run, shout, and tell the whole world.

I offered the factory's gatekeeper a cigarette, and rather uncharacteristically gave a beggar a few coins. I then went to the grocers and from there to the barbers. As I was being shaved I was getting impatient. I must have been fidgeting under his razor, because he stopped.

"Please, sir! Could you calm down? We're going to have an accident!"

"Oh? You think that's a possibility?"

The barber gave me a strange look.

"Do you honestly think," I explained, "that your razor would be so heartless as to cut the cheek of the happiest man on earth?"

The barber let out a short laugh.

"My, my," he said, "Someone's very happy. What happened, did you win the lottery?"

I wasn't going to wait for the wash, the talc, the cream, anything...

"I couldn't care less about all the lotteries in the world!" I shouted, as I ran out of his shop.

The barber called out after me.

"Your Excellency has forgotten to pay!"

"Oh! Oh, I do beg his Majesty's pardon..." I said, turning back sharply.

I then went into the cellar behind the grocer's. I sat down to eat some pastrami, some pickles, a few black olives, and a quarter-loaf of bread... And to dive into some wine. 'All on my tab, please, Master Grocer,' obviously...

I downed one glass, then another. Ahh! Then, as I was about to start eating the generous portion of pastrami, I hesitated. It would probably make my breath smell, and that might make her uncomfortable. I would not allow her to feel uncomfortable, whatever the cause! The factory working hours would soon be over, and I would be waiting for her at the window. She would come out laughing, glance over at me, walk past there, right there, laugh, and glance over again. I placed a huge pickled gherkin into my mouth, and bit down with my strong teeth. My crooked nose and skinny fingers didn't enter my thoughts. In any case, I had been putting on weight since I'd started work. But forget about all that... I was over the moon. I had only just realised how sweet an effect wine can have on you. Where's that sad, inner me? Nowhere to be found. Hiding. I felt so powerful, the inner me dared not show his face.

Any time now, she would come out, glance over, laugh, turn back, glance over, laugh, turn, glance over... Then time would move on, the moon would come out, I'd go over to their neighbourhood, into that street, into that smell of sewage, and be under her window... Life is brilliant, absolutely brilliant!

When the workers left the factory she did too. As

usual, she glanced over, smiled, and gave a little signal. I understood.

The hours passed very slowly. Eventually, as the clock in the tower struck nine, I entered the disgustingly smelly street. Her window was dark. I moved in closer. And there at the window, no more than a dark silhouette, stood my beloved.

"You're late," she whispered down.

"Who, me?"

"Yes, you!"

"But it's only nine o'clock! Is that too late?"

"Well, maybe not... Anyway, what did that woman say to you?"

"Which one?"

"That mad old one. Her name's Gullu."

"Oh, the one I spoke to over by the corner..."

"Yes, her."

"'That girl has many men after her,' she said. 'You'd better give up on her. They'll shoot you, they'll kill you,' she said. She told me the men after you were rich enough to pay out my weight in gold!"

"So she said that, eh? Why, the... And then?"

"Well, just that there were many men after you. That your dad was a difficult man, and that there was no way he'd let someone like me marry you..."

"And when she said all this to you...?"

"I believed her. I assumed you knew she..."

"No, I had no idea! So, that's why you lost interest in me?"

"What was I to think?"

"Look, I'm not blinded by gold or diamonds. You listen to me. From now on, I want to see you there every day, at the cellar window, waiting for me. I want you to be there!"

"Do you really?"

"Really truly!"

"Who is that woman anyway?"

"No-one, really. Just a friend. But she cares for me a lot... Do come over when my father goes to evening prayers, and we can talk, OK?"

"Well, OK, but how will I know when he's going to go?"

"I'll let you know."

"Write a little note."

"I don't know how to read or write..."

"Well, then send over the little girl..."

"You make sure you sit at the window, now. Just look at me the way you do, and smile. The other girls get so jealous... Let them, the tarts, serves them right!"

"Maybe we could go to the pictures one day...?"

"To the pictures? Are you mad?"

"Why?"

"That's impossible!"

"Well, OK then, but why?"

"My father would kill me!"

"So your father really is..."

"Do you have a mother? They told me about your father. Apparently he's not here, is he? Why is he in exile?"

"It's a long story."

"Who do you stay with? Why didn't you go with him?"

"I did go, at first, but then I came back. I'm living with my grandmother."

"Listen, you wait for me by that window every day, OK? Then, and I'll let you know when, you can have your grandmother come over to ours and ask for me, OK?"

"...?"

"OK?"

"Alright..."

"Well, you'd better go now; my father will be back soon... But don't forget, I want you waiting by that window, right?"

It was a sparklingly brilliant night, the city was asleep,

and the roads were quiet and dusty...

Before long, the whole thing had spread around the factory like wildfire. Before I knew what had happened I had received four written death threats, one after another.

They were going to kill me! I was told that I had to give up on that girl, and that there were plenty of girls in office work. Or else. Signed by: The Black Crows!

And at the bottom, pictures of a dagger dripping blood, a smoking pistol, and a pair of clenched fists. But, in spite of it all, I went to the window of the wine cellar every afternoon. Now and then the little girl would come, and tell me that 'her sister' would wait for me that night. I had to walk through many deserted streets to get to hers. One of the streets led through an empty park. But I wasn't afraid. It all seemed like a big game.

"I'm afraid!" she confided in me one night. "I keep having these terrible, terrible dreams. I am so worried they're going to shoot you!"

"Well, what can I do?"

"That's up to you, really. You should have your grandmother come over..."

"...?"

"Well, if she doesn't, you'll lose me!"

"Why? What's happening?

"I think my father's got wind of something. He wants me to go over and stay at my uncle's, in Sivas. And the other day, someone threw stones at our window. I'm very frightened. If my father found out for sure..."

"So, I'll have to get my grandmother to come over. What if your father doesn't agree?"

"Well, at least get her to ask him..."

A few days later, Gullu came to the factory.

"This evening," she said to me, "come over to ours."

"Yours? I don't know where you live!"

"We're two doors down from your girl. Just come over, don't worry, I'll wait for you by the door. Make sure you come, this is important!"

At nine o'clock that evening, I went to the woman's house. She was waiting for me by the door. We went in, and climbed up four rotting old wooden steps. We entered a small room. Its windows had been papered over. A man, who turned out to be her husband and a construction worker, welcomed me in, shook my hand, and offered me a cigarette. Gullu made us coffee.

"That day," she said, "I was testing you. But, there really are a lot of young men after the girl. The trouble is things have got out of hand now. Someone's been sending her father letters, and he's been in a complete rage, and he's attacking the poor girl. He beat her last night for hours, with a big stick, and the poor girl's covered in bruises. The girl didn't tell him your name, but he's going to find out sooner or later."

"If you don't hurry up," said her husband, "and get your family around there to ask for her, she's going to be sent to Sivas, to live at her uncle's. Either that, or the man will kill the pair of you. You know how it is..."

And he told me a story.

Back where they came from, a Moslem girl once ran off to marry a young Christian man. The Christians celebrated. The Moslems were beside themselves with rage. At the time, my girl's father had been out in the mountains. When he found out, he set a trap. When the boy and the girl got in to bed on their wedding night my girl's father crept up to their window and, just as they were kissing, shot them both with one bullet...

I came back home, dazed and confused. My grandmother was sitting down. Where would I start? How could I tell her? I knew that she would...

"What's on your mind this time?" she asked, "Lost all your ships at sea?"

"I'm not happy."

"Why on earth not? You're not hungry, and you're not naked, thank God... What's there to be unhappy about?"

"Oh, I don't know. I'm feeling really restless. I don't

know what to do..."

"You've been drinking again. Why don't you just stop drinking that stuff?"

It was now or never.

"I can't help it. You know why I drink like this?"

She looked at me slyly.

"No, why do you drink like this? Tell me, then I'll understand!"

"I drink because I'm lonely. I work all day, I get tired, and all I get to do in the evening is to sit in this dingy room."

"And... What do you want me to do about it?"

I laughed. She laughed too.

"Go on," she said, "spit it out!"

I laughed again.

"You have to spell it out, son. We can't find a solution unless we know the exact problem!"

I laughed again, and started pacing up and down the room. I felt as if I was locked in by her stare.

"Who is she?" she finally asked, "Is she from a good family, at least?"

I could have died.

"Look," I managed to say, "I haven't even finished middle school myself. You know I can't get someone in a high position. The girl I want is..."

"Why do you belittle yourself so much? There's nothing wrong with you, is there? I know your salary isn't much, but still... And anyway, you haven't done your military service yet. What about your mother and father? Are they going to agree to this?"

She was perfectly right, of course, but...

"So, who is she? Where does her family come from? What's their background, who are they? I certainly don't want you with any old loose woman..."

"Oh, no. They're very honourable. And..."

"So who is she?"

"She works over where I do..."

"At the office?"

"No..."

"Where then?"

"At the factory..."

"What? A common labourer! Oh my God, what have I done to deserve this? Are you mad, boy? Have you lost your mind? Working in a factory, among all those men; She'll have been through dozens of them! Heavens preserve us!"

She mumbled angrily to herself as she got up, washed, and prepared for her prayers at sundown.

I ran out into the street.

XIX

The days wouldn't pass.

No matter how much I begged, my grandmother would not budge.

"You need money to get married. Where's your money? When your wife turns around and asks you for something, you won't be able to provide it. You'll end up a bitter and resentful man. You haven't even done your military service yet! Where's your wife going to stay when you're off in the army? Then, and more importantly, there's your father, your mother, your brother and your sisters... It's hardly appropriate for you to set yourself up in comfort when they're in the state they're in..."

My grandmother was absolutely right.

My beloved was absolutely right, too.

And me? Was I wrong?

I found myself caught in the cogs of a giant machine, being inexorably pulled this way and that. I became unable to get to sleep unless I was drunk enough to be oblivious to everything. If I did accidentally go to bed without drinking quite enough, the inner me would rise up, and get into an endless argument with me about how this would lead to that, and that would result in the other. Should I sacrifice my father, mother, brother and sisters, or my beloved? When I fell asleep, I often dreamt of my father.

"What kind of a son are you?" he'd be saying to me, "Shame on you! Here we are, in this desperate poverty, and you're off doing all that..."

I dreamt of the whole family. How they had lost weight, how sunken their eyes were, how pale and ashen they looked...

I would wake with a start. The inner "me" would fan the flames. "You're a real lowlife," he would tell me. Just then my beloved would enter the conversation, with her clean white face and beautiful dark eyes.

"Everyone is talking about me because of you! You've embarrassed me in front of everybody! What's to become of me now?"

Yes, what is to become of you now? And what's to become of my father, my mother, my brother, my sisters, me, you... What is to become of us?

I saw her in a dream one night.

She was lying on the floor of a dark basement, hands and feet bound tightly together. A small bulb in the far corner was giving off a pale yellow light. Her father was angrily sharpening a huge, broad knife. My beloved was reaching out to me, pleading...

I woke up with a scream. I was covered in sweat.

"What on earth's the matter, son?" asked my grandmother, "What's worrying you? Look at the state you're in!"

"It's nothing..."

"Bad dreams?"

"Yes..."

"What happened?"

"I don't know..."

"How could you not know? Something made you scream out loud!"

"I don't know..."

I continued to receive letters threatening to kill me, each one more vicious than the last.

XX

"Her father," said the Bosnian woman, Gullu, "He's going to beat that poor girl to death! If you don't get a move on, he may send her off to Sivas, to her uncle's..."

Her husband was sitting on the floor.

"Why don't you send your Nan over to ask for you to be married? What are you waiting for?" he asked.

Could I possible tell them about the factory slut, the cast-off of dozens of other men? They had invited me over to wrap the matter up tonight, to bring it all to a sound conclusion. Either this was going to have to go ahead and happen, or I was going to have to clearly put a stop to it all.

I was desperate. So I lied.

"I have written to my father," I said, "and I'm waiting for his reply. That's all it is..."

"Did you ask for money?"

"No. We have these fields, you see. So I asked for a Power of Attorney. As soon as that comes through..."

"What's that?" asked Gullu's husband, "You have fields?"

"We do..."

"Many? Where? On good soil?"

I told him their location, and size. He got quite excited.

"Goodness me," he said, "Did you hear that? So you have that much land? But why don't you farm it?"

I went through a whole story. He listened carefully.

"Listen, young man," he said, "You put all of us together, and we can do it. There's me, there's my wife, there's you, there's your girl, your girl's brother, her father..."

He told me how we could build up a lovely farm. We could have cows, chicken, sheep and goats, so we would have plenty of eggs and milk. Some of the land could be used for growing fruit and vegetables. In time, the cows, chicken and sheep would increase, and we could get into selling butter, milk and eggs. Gradually business could expand...

"Just get your letter," said Gullu's husband, "and I won't ask you for a penny! We can go and build us a nice little homestead with our very own hands. I'll bring in five or six chicken, a cockerel, plant some lemon and orange trees, and some vegetables, and we'll be set. I'm sick of laying bricks!"

Gullu was as keen as he was. The two of them came up with such ideas, encouraging each other as they went on, that even though I knew that their talk was completely unrealistic I found myself caught up in their excitement. I decided that the very next day, I would genuinely write to my father and ask for a Power of Attorney.

They thought of the whole thing as being settled already. Gullu was so happy that she got up, and came over clutching a huge quilting-needle.

"So, young man," she said, "are you up for it?"

"What?"

"Be my blood brother?"

"Yes, why not?" I found myself saying.

Her husband intervened.

"We can't just do that without celebrating... Let me go and get some brandy, and some lemonade, and we can have a toast. Then..."

Gullu flung her arms around her husband's neck in delight.

"This is great!" she said, kissing him, "I'm so excited! Hang on," she added, turning to me, "I just thought of something... Shall I go and bring your girl over?"

"But you have to behave yourself," added her husband, "don't go and ruin everything!"

Gullu had run off, and was already out of the door. So when her husband left to get the brandy and the lemonade, I was left alone in their room. I stared out at the night sky through their window. A red moon was slowly rising in the far distance, a whispery sound was drifting over from the factory, and a slowly rumbling machine was standing in as the heartbeat for the whole neighbourhood.

I felt uncomfortable, heavy in my heart. I couldn't quite put my finger on it. Yet my beloved would be here in a minute, we'd probably sit side by side, maybe even exchange looks and smiles. I suddenly noticed the cupboard in the room, and that its door was ajar. I went over and looked in. It was full of books. I was surprised. They certainly couldn't have belonged to Gullu or her husband. I wondered whose they were. I wondered what they were about. Who put them there? I had just reached in to pull one out at random, when the front door opened, and loudly slammed shut. I edged away from the cupboard.

It was Gullu, returning in the same mad rush she had left in.

"I've got permission," she said, "so she'll be over in a minute. But you must sit nicely! I don't want any hanky panky... I lied to her father, and he bought it. I said we're going to have a drink of sherbet at Beyto's. If it was anyone else, he'd have said 'no,' believe me! But for me... Well, he'll do anything for me. Loves me like his own daughter. But if only my brother were here... Now him, he'd die for! If only he was here..."

"Your brother?" I asked, "Who's he?"

"He isn't around anymore... He's very clever, is my brother. Knows all these long words... You could sit and listen to him all day."

She opened the door to the cupboard I had just been looking at.

"See all these books? They're his. He read every night..."

My curiosity was piqued.

"Where is he now?"

"He's not around anymore. He left."

"Where did he go?"

"I don't know. He just left... He used to work at the cloth factory, you know. Used to be a master weaver..."

My jaw dropped.

"What's his name?"

"Izzet. Master Izzet, they called him. Hang on, look, I've got a picture somewhere…"

She went and fetched the picture of her brother from the adjacent room. Hey, it was him! It was my friend with the blue overalls!

"Hey, I know him," I exclaimed, "He's a friend of mine!"

Gullu came over all serious suddenly, and looked me up and down.

"You do? Hmm… Do you have books too?"

"I do…"

"Many?"

"A few."

She shook her head.

"So he's your friend, eh? Well, if he's your friend, why are you having to ask where he is?"

Her husband came in with the brandy and lemonade.

"Look," she said to him, "what a small world it is. He knows my brother. He's a friend of his."

She took the bottles off her husband.

"Really?" he said, "He's a friend of yours, eh?"

The couple exchanged looks, had a chuckle, and winked at each other.

"What's up?" I asked, "What's there to be surprised about? What's the joke? Why are you winking? It's not that weird; I only said I knew him!"

"No," said Gullu, "of course it isn't."

I came out with loads of questions about him, and although I wanted to get to know something about him, I failed. They seemed to want to close the subject, as if they may be trying to hide something from me.

"Did Izzet have a wife and children?" I asked.

"He did," said Gullu, "he had a wife. Worked in the factory with us, she did. But she got her arm caught in one of the machines, lost a lot of blood, and died.

"She died?"

"She died."

"And the children?"

"There was one. Got run over by a train."

"What?"

"He died under a train."

"Bloody hell! How did that happen? How old was the child?"

"Only six. Lovely little boy. Thick, curly hair, stout kid, bright as anything…

"But how did it happen? How did he end up under a train?"

"Well, his mum had to be at work, and his dad was in prison at the time…"

"In prison? Why?"

"Oh, nothing interesting," said Gullu's husband, "stealing chickens, as it happens."

"The train was going along," continued Gullu, "and he was playing on the rails. Poor little mite fell over, and his little foot got stuck. He wanted to get away, but couldn't. Got sliced in half. Not wanting to sound morbid, but right across here, like that… They brought him back in two pieces."

I saw the image of Master Izzet, watching me.

"This neighbourhood," he'd said to me, "and I'll say this in words you'd use, is a neighbourhood of people that God forgot. There are plenty of others, with far greater rights to complain than you have!"

"Have you ever seen a cut-off arm?" asked Gullu's husband, "It wiggles and wiggles like this. And the fingers open and close, and it turns purple…"

"I have," said Gullu, "there was this man Suleyman; he used to fluff up wool. An Arab, he was, with dark bushy hair. It was his wife… Her arm got ripped off right next to me. I was shocked! I picked up her arm, and held it. It was all warm, and dripping blood…"

I suddenly felt quite sick. I had visions of cut off

fingers and arms, wiggling at me. I felt I could almost hear the noise made by the warm blood gushing out of the veins.

Then, my beloved turned up. She seemed sulky.

"I'm waiting for a Power of Attorney to come through by post!" I told her.

"Why? What good is that? Or did you ask him to give you money?"

"I asked him for a Power of Attorney," I repeated, "Power of Attorney?"

She shrugged.

"What's the use of that?"

I went into the details of the now definite plans for the farm we were going to have with Gullu. Gullu and her husband backed me up too. My beloved seemed to believe me.

"I just hope," she said, "that things don't all go wrong before all that comes through."

And she explained: Her father was really pressuring her, people were stopping her on her way to and from work, and pulling knives on her. She was getting death threats, and people were stoning their windows at night.

Gullu handed her a glass full of brandy and lemonade.

"Go on girl," she said, "get that down you. Bottoms up! I don't want to see anything left in that glass, or else!"

My beloved drained the glass.

Then, I drank. Then, Gullu and her husband drank. So it went on, glasses being topped up and emptied. After a while, when we were all quite drunk, Gullu returned with her quilting-needle.

"Watch," she said, "I'll prick myself first, and then it'll be your turn! Ready?"

She stuck the needle in. A large drop of red blood hovered on the end of her finger. She held it out to me. I sucked it. Then I pricked my finger, and she sucked that. So now, I was officially her blood-brother.

Gullu's husband was now very drunk too. To celebrate

tonight, he went and got his harmonica. It seems that the harmonica had stayed in their cupboard since the day master Izzet had lost his son. Today, for the first time since that fateful day, he was going to play it in my honour.

So that night we played music, we sang, and we laughed. Gullu sang us Bosnian folk-songs, and she and her husband danced for us.

My beloved rested her head on my shoulder. I put my arm around her slim waist, which nonetheless felt full of life. I must have squeezed a touch too hard because she let out a little yelp, and looked towards Gullu and her husband.

"Don't be rude," she said to me, "there's people around!"

Gullu must have noticed, because she quickly blew out the lamp. The sudden darkness slowly gave way to the strong, silvery light of the moon, streaming through the window. It gleamed and scattered on the metal inlays of Gullu's wooden chest.

Gullu and her husband had started a new folk dance, a livelier one, and were spinning in sudden, vigorous moves.

I grabbed hold of my beloved, and pulled her to me with all my strength.

Suddenly, there was furious banging at the street door. My beloved slipped down away from me, almost flowing out of my arms. She was clearly terrified. She had frozen by my feet, unable to get up or move.

"It's my father," she said, "that's my father. He must have heard that I hadn't gone to drink sherbet. Oh God, what have I done? What am I going to do now?"

Gullu quickly re-lit the lamp, and her husband put the bottles away.

"Come on," he said, "if it's your father, it's your father! So what? What's he going to do?"

He went to the door.

I held my beloved's hands. They had gone ice cold.

"What will we do?" she kept saying, "What will we do? He'll kill me now!"

Suddenly we heard loud, joyous Bosnian exclamations, laughter and shouting.

"It's my brother!" said Gullu, "It is, it's him!"

She leapt away.

It really was her brother. He staggered tiredly into the room, where he saw me.

"Well well! Look who's here! Goodness me, what are you doing here?"

We shook hands. Gullu and her husband told him all about what I was doing there. Master Izzet listened attentively and looked serious. But he did not ask any questions.

"Sister," he said to Gullu, "would you mind heating up a pan of water for me?"

Gullu got up immediately, and went to put some water on. Master Izzet sat silently for a minute, while he smoked his cigarette.

"You'll have to excuse me," he said, "I'm too tired now. We'll talk tomorrow. I'll be here for a while now, anyway."

He left us.

"Where do you know him from?" asked my beloved, "He's a very good friend of my father's. But how do you know him?"

I told her.

"Well, that's good, then..." she said, "You try and convince him about us. He's my father's greatest friend in the world!"

Gullu's husband had put his harmonica away. He was smoking a cigarette. Then he got up too, and we were left alone. I held my beloved in my arms again, but she pulled back this time. Her white headscarf slipped down onto her neck, and she was blushing furiously.

"Stop it," she said, "Please, let go. I need to ask you something."

I let go.

"Fire away!" I said.

"But you have to answer truthfully!"

"I will."

"Hope to die if you don't?"

"Hope to die if I don't."

"Right… So, why haven't you had your family come over to ask for me?"

She had got me right where it hurt.

"I'm going to," I said.

"That night," she said, "You promised you would get your grandmother to come over. What happened?"

"Well, as I said, I've written to my father…"

"You didn't say anything about writing to your father before. You said that you were going to talk to your grandmother, and get her to come and ask. Hmm? Why didn't she come?"

"…?"

"Why don't you answer? Did you ask her, and she wouldn't come? Did she say 'How could I ask for a factory girl to marry my grandson'?"

I felt as if boiling water had been poured over my head.

"Oh no," I said, "it was nothing like that."

"Oh, no, it was exactly something like that, wasn't it? I know those sort of people. They wouldn't stoop to a factory girl. They'd say 'she would have slept with thousands of men,' and refuse to lower themselves."

I tried to hush her.

"No, don't try and stop me!" she said, "Leave me alone! I know what those people are like. Your grandmother refused to come and ask for me so you… Look, I want you to be honest with me. You can't be hiding anything from me. And anyway, you've nothing to be embarrassed about. It's true, isn't it? Hm? Isn't that what she said?"

I felt awful.

"Hey, I'm talking to you, answer me! That's it, isn't it?

She's a factory girl, not good enough for our family, she'll have been with thousands of men, that's what she said, isn't it? Talk to me!"

Suddenly, she took hold of my hand.

"Look at me... Forget about them. Do you love me, or not?"

"I love you a lot..."

"So then, don't wait on any money from your father..."

"It's not money; it's a Power of Attorney..."

"Whatever. Don't ask for anything. You talk to my father. You could come around one evening, and ask for me... My father's a tough man, and he appreciates bravery and honesty. So don't worry; come over to ours, and tell him..."

"What if he chases me away?"

"He won't. Don't worry about the things people say about him, he's not a bad man. He likes straight talk. So you come and ask for me yourself, and forget about other people doing it..."

"If he says no?"

"You just ask. If he says no, we'll worry about it then. My brother's heard about us, and apparently he knows you because of you playing football, and admires you a lot. He's already said good things about you to my father. So don't you worry. You come over, ask for me, I'm sure he'll say yes. My father's an honest man, and he likes honesty."

Then she went into a lengthy explanation: We didn't need money. She wouldn't ask me for shoes, or clothes, or what not. As for my salary, yes, I didn't earn much, and it wouldn't be enough for the two of us. But she would be working too. We could hire a single room here in their courtyard, settle there, and that would be that! If two hearts were together, what else mattered?"

"I do want to ask you something, though," she said, "Did you love anyone before me? Have you been with other women at all?"

"No, never."

"Tell me the truth…"

"I am telling the truth."

"I don't believe you," she said, "You must have been with other women!"

Finally, I talked about the Greek girl Eleni in Beirut. She listened attentively.

"She must have been prettier than I am," she said, "Come on, be honest. I mean, whatever is past, is past. All sorts of things happen when you're young. But now…?"

"Nothing like that could happen now."

"It better not!"

"What would you do?"

"What would I do? You'd find out…"

Then she questioned me about my father and my family.

"Why did they go there? Who looks after them? Why don't they come over? Couldn't they come, if they wanted?"

I talked about them briefly, and explained that my brother Niyazi looked after them now.

"Is he younger than you?"

"He is. About five years."

"Five years younger? Good on him. What does he do?"

"Sells things on the street. Well, to be honest, he does whatever work he can find."

"So he's one of us, then? If I'd been you, I wouldn't have left my mum and dad to come here."

As I couldn't think of a way to explain my reasoning at the time, I kept silent.

"I can do lacework, really ornate things, and I can knit. I won't be a burden to you. Come on, come over and ask for me. My father won't bite!"

By the time I left, it was very late. I felt happy and at peace, as if I had everything a man could want. The streets were deserted. The lights were all off in people's homes.

Shops' shutters were all shut...

Although I tried desperately not to wake my grandmother up, a floorboard creaked under my foot and, naturally, my grandmother was up like a shot. She asked me where I had been. I told her.

"Oh you crazy boy," she said, "you crazy boy... A girl brought up among a thousand men. You're going to regret this, but..."

I talked to her for a long time.

"No, no, no..." she said, "I'll not have anything to do with it. If God lets it happen, it'll be his doing. I don't want to know."

She pulled her quilt over her head.

I went to bed. For the first time in weeks, I had a long, uninterrupted sleep. That night I dreamt of a sunny orange grove full of sparkling golden birds, with a glittering silver stream running through it.

XXI

"Your grandmother is absolutely right!" said Master Izzet.

I objected immediately.

"What? She's right? How can you say that?"

"Yes, she's right," he interrupted, "Firstly, you haven't the money to get married. Secondly, you don't earn enough. And thirdly – and this is probably the most important point of all..."

"What's that?"

"You have got to accept what the people around you are going to think. As far as they're concerned, a girl working in a factory cannot possibly be honest and decent."

"But..."

"I said, you have to accept that this is what they think! I'm not saying they're right, obviously. I'm only trying to explain their point of view. This is what they will think, and such thoughts are their handicap. They will also be unaware that such attitudes are their handicap. But sooner or later you will be with this poor girl in their environment. And those people will look down on this girl, as if she had slept around with other men. They will talk about her behind her back, and make snide remarks... That'll upset both her and you. In due course she will fit in, though, and start to copy them. She'll dress like them, talk like them, and start to think like them. Then one day, she will become ashamed of having worked in a factory and of her humble past, and be miserable for the rest of her life."

He looked at me carefully.

"I won't let that happen!" I said.

"Well, there's nothing else I can say," he said, "It's quite clear that you have made up your mind, and that you're not about to change it. So let's drop the subject. You see...".

And he told me all about my beloved.

"She is a lovely girl: A very dutiful daughter. She works twelve hours in the factory, and then comes back home and scrubs the floors, does the laundry, mends the clothes, darns the socks... She is a sound girl. She will keep your house going single-handedly! Nonetheless, the day will come when you will regret ever marrying her. I repeat: You have an inquisitive nature, and you're intelligent. One day, you're going to realise the consequences of what you've done, and rue this day. I don't know..."

That was all we said on the subject. I think it was about three days later, he left as abruptly as he'd arrived. I had no idea why or where he went. But he did me another great kindness before he left: He talked to my prospective father-in-law, and told him about me, and in particular, about my father. Apparently the old man smiled when he heard my father's name. He'd known him well from their partisan days.

"For his son," he apparently said, "I'd give five

daughters, if I had them, let alone the one!"

I was taken aback.

"But Master Izzet," I said, "I'll be the one marrying his daughter, not my father! I don't want him to get the wrong idea…"

"Well," he said, "You can straighten that part out yourself. We're going to go to their place tomorrow, so be ready. Come and find me at the Cretan's café at seven!"

We met up the following evening. I was overjoyed. I had just had the perfect shave, slicked my hair down, and my heart was pounding with hope and excitement. We set off down the dusty roads. The sun had set. There was no moonlight. The sky was full of dark clouds, and it was windy. We passed through the narrow, winding streets, past the windows overlooking them, past the laughter, the noises from gramophones, the drunken shouts and the watchmen's whistles, and arrived at the courtyard of my beloved. She was waiting for us by the courtyard door with her arms folded firmly over her hands. She showed us in. We entered the courtyard. The dark courtyard was covered in small, muddy puddles, and stank. As we walked past the rented rooms, we noticed curious shadows, and heard their whisperings. The residents certainly knew what was going on!

My prospective father-in-law greeted us with a toothless smile. We went up the four steps inside their door. We emerged into a small room which was immaculately clean and had snow-white walls. A lantern with a sparklingly clean glass was illuminating the room. Gullu and her husband had arrived before us, and had sat down in the most prominent position in the room. Gullu was giggling non-stop.

My prospective father-in-law scrutinised me all night long. He talked all about my father, about the Party, and about the speeches my father had made. I talked about this and that, mostly about Beirut and Antakya.

My beloved got up and made coffee for us. Then, in

her nervousness, she tripped and spilt it all over the floor! She got very embarrassed at this, and ran off out of the room. So anyway, what with one thing or another, time passed. We drank freshly made coffee, smoked our cigarettes, and when we were all done, and all that was left in the room was the smoke from the cigarettes, we came to the serious matter at hand. My prospective father-in-law became serious, and went into a "Well, the son of a great man like that…" phase.

"Just one minute!" I said.

Everyone turned to stare at me. They must have wondered what on earth I would come up with. As for me, I went and came up with such an astounding and pathetic story, full of everything down to the twenty-four liras and ninety-five kurus, that my father-in-law to be leapt up, and kissed me on the forehead.

"God bless you son!" he said, "You can have my daughter with my blessings! And I don't want a thing; Just pick her up, and carry her off!"

So that was it then. I had the horse, and I had three horseshoes. As for the fourth horseshoe… Well, we'd sort something out, eh?

XXII

How on earth did my grandmother agree to it?

You know, I still have no idea.

She agreed. I told her how to get to their home. So she went, and saw the girl.

"What do you think?" I asked.

"Not bad," she said. "She had a pair of black pants on, and she was doing their laundry. She seems hard-working, pretty, and home-loving. But I'm not sure…"

We first had a simple and embarrassing engagement (embarrassing because our engagement rings were only simple copper bands) and later, we had our wedding.

XXIII

Hasan Hussein borrowed a navy suit for me to wear on the day. Gazi got hold of a new razor-blade, and managed to borrow a pair of patent leather shoes and a tie for me. I was getting married, and I had exactly forty five kurus, half a packet of village cigarettes, and eighteen kurus-worth of cooperative tokens.

Long live freedom!

"Hey, Hasan Hussein," said Gazi, "I only have one-and-a-half liras. What about you?"

Hasan Hussein gulped.

"What me? I've got thirty-five kurus."

"And you, mister bridegroom?"

"I have forty-five kurus..."

"Hey, so I'm the richest, eh? Now look here mate, I have a hundred and fifty, Hasan's got thirty-five, that's a hundred and eighty-five. Now you've got another forty-five, so that's... Well, you're the accountant, what's that make?"

"Two hundred and thirty!" said Hasan Hussein.

"Two hundred and thirty? No, hang on. Forget that last forty-five, the idiot here is getting a wife – he might need that. Take away forty-five from two hundred and thirty?"

"One hundred and eighty-five..."

"One hundred and eighty-five, right. You know what we're going to do now? We're going to dive into the Cretan's cellar, and we're going to get drunk in honour of the idiot who's getting himself another mouth to feed!"

"Gazi, you know," said Hasan Hussein, "Sometimes you come up with flashes of absolute genius!"

So we dived into the Cretan's cellar, where (back then, in 1937) wine was sold at five kurus a glass. Everyone filled their own glass from the huge barrel. Gazi lifted up his glass.

"To the idiot who, tonight, gets himself an extra mouth to feed!"

So we clinked our glasses together, and emptied them

in one go.

"Bloody hell," said Hasan Hussein, "I mean, look at you! Navy suit, patent-leather shoes, shirt and tie, you look like a right gentleman! Very smart, my man! You look here, mate, I want no showing off in front of the missus, though... I swear I'll dive in there and tell her that the suit and shoes and everything are all borrowed. Don't come over all posh on her!"

"Don't you worry, mate," I said, "she's already got the measure of me!"

"Oh yeah?"

"I told her all about my twenty-four liras and ninety-five kurus, and everything..."

Gazi wrapped me in his arms, and kissed me on the cheek.

"Don't get upset, mate," he said, "This'll all be behind us soon enough. One day, we'll be telling our kids what great men we were!"

We toasted this, drank to that, and ended up quite drunk. We couldn't see across the cellar for cigarette smoke, and our laughter cut through the air and exploded like fireworks. Then the old wine merchant joined us too, smiling under his white moustache, and started drinking. A short time later his large nose went red, and his eyes became swollen. As he raised his glass for a toast, his wife stormed into the cellar. Her fists were resting firmly on her wide hips.

"My, my, my!" she said, "So you're here too! We have customers waiting for service, and you're there drinking with these kids. You ought to be ashamed of yourself! At your age..."

The large old man raised his glass to toast his fateful day, thirty-five years ago.

"Hurrah!" he shouted, "Bless you, lads!"

By rights, we had six-and-a-half glasses each, but they let me have their extra half-glass, so I'd drunk over seven glasses.

We left together, and they brought me home.

My beloved met me at the door. She was all dressed up, and covered in laces, embroidery and sequins. My head was spinning. They were playing music, and women, girls and children were hurrying around. I felt ill...

They ushered me into a room prepared specially for the day. Chairs and divans, carpets and kilims, decorated walls, colourful dresses on hangers... All this was simply not possible on the fifty liras that I'd somehow managed to get the factory to advance me, but still...

I let myself flop down onto a chair.

"They're about to present the wedding gifts to me," said my beloved, "so make sure you listen in... Look, all these carpets, kilims and dresses – they're all ours!"

"Huh?"

They called my beloved away, so off she went.

I was at a loss to fathom how this had all come about.

A little later an old woman's voice came through the door, loud and clear.

"One beautiful gold bracelet, from the boy's father. Wear it in good times!"

"From his mother, a necklace. May it bring you good fortune!"

"One pair of fine bangles!"

"A beautiful pair of diamond earrings!"

"One carpet, tufted at both ends!"

"...!"

"...!"

"...!"

I couldn't really get my head together, but I was aware that a small fortune was being put our way. That means that my father, my mother, all our relatives... Whereas I...

I passed out. When I came to, my beloved was in front of me. Someone was hammering at the insides of my skull.

"Look!" she said, "See all these things they put on me? Look at all these bracelets and bangles! And look at this necklace! And what about these earrings? They've got diamonds! These must add up to five or six-hundred lira's worth! Gullu says...

"What does Gullu say?"

"She says we should sell some of these after a while, and that'll be a start-up capital for you, and then you can have your own business. She's right. We won't be dependent on other people then, eh?"

"Yeah... I could open up a restaurant... Or maybe..."

"Or maybe you could have a café, or a nice clean grocery shop. I like the earrings best."

"So all these were presents?"

"They were... Your relatives were very kind... And you'd been telling me..."

"I must have got the wrong end of the stick, I guess..."

"Look at these kilims! And what about the carpets?"

"Is this dress material yours too?"

"Yes! And those dresses... I'll not be wanting any new clothes from you for years!"

"So, we've done pretty well out of this, eh?"

"We've done very well. But whatever happens, let's not get carried away with spending, OK? And you can stop drinking all that wine. I won't be idle, either. We can buy a sewing machine by instalments, I'll learn how to sew, and I can work as a seamstress and earn some money as well..."

I opened my eyes the next day, and my beloved was standing in front of the mirror. I quietly sat up in the bed. I took a good look at her. She was combing her hair, plaiting it and putting it in clips. Then she tried on some lipstick, and powdered her face. She picked up the earrings, kissed them, and put them on. She admired herself, turning to one side, then the other. Then she turned right round, looked at her back and suddenly noticed me. She shrieked, hid her face in her hands, and threw herself onto the bed, right next to me. I held her hand and lifted her up.

"What's the matter, hmm? What are you embarrassed about?"

She was bright red all the way to her earlobes.

"Tell me... Why are you embarrassed? Eh?"

She didn't answer, and wouldn't look me in the eyes.

"You know," she said after a while, looking at me with her big, dark eyes, "I really love these earrings! Let's sell these last, or not sell them at all!"

"OK... We won't sell them at all."

"First we can cash in the bangles, then the necklace, and later... You know what I'm going to do? I'm going to put on lipstick, I'm going to powder my face, I'm going to put on all my jewellery, I'm going to look just perfect, and I'm going to take you by the arm, and I'm going to walk all through the neighbourhood! I bet my friends will be so jealous when they see me like this. Don't you think?"

"Of course..."

"Let them get jealous, the tarts! Wouldn't come to my wedding, would they? Gullu says to put it all on and let them all see. Let the tarts go mad, she says. Ooh, can we have a photo taken too? We can send it to my uncle. Will you look at these earrings? Oh, they're so lovely! They do suit me, don't they?"

"Everything suits you, my gorgeous!"

Two days later, my grandmother pulled me over to one side.

"Son," she said, "You know it's our family tradition, and you know I had to keep up appearances for the sake of your father. You tell your wife in a way you think is best..."

"What's that?"

"The things I borrowed..."

"What things?"

"All that gold jewellery: the bracelet, the earrings, the bangles, the necklace..."

"What?"

"We need to return them..."

"What? You borrowed all that? They all belong to other people?"

"What could I do? One's got to keep up appearances…"

I felt as if someone had shot me.

"Curse you, and your traditions!" I said, "Screw the lot of you! You want your wedding gifts back? You go and ask her! Do your own dirty work; I've already sunk as low as I'm going to, because of you lot! I won't do it!"

I stormed out.

That evening my wife was waiting for me at the top of the stairs. She had none of the jewellery on. No earrings, no necklace, no bangles. We went into our room. We stood in the room, facing each other.

"I want to say something," she said, after a while, "but I don't want you to get upset. Please promise me you won't be angry or upset!"

I pretended not to understand.

"Why, what's the matter?"

"No, please," she repeated, "promise me you won't get upset!"

"OK, OK… Just tell me what it is, I'll be fine…"

"Do you notice anything missing?"

"Such as?"

"Look at my ears!"

"Oh, yeah… Where are your earrings?"

She threw her arms around my neck. Her eyes were brimming with tears.

"Please don't get cross… Don't upset yourself; we're both young, we'll work, and we'll earn money, and we'll make it on our own. It's not as if we were born with diamond earrings!"

"You still haven't told me what happened…"

"Your grandmother came and took everything back. She'd apparently borrowed them all from friends and neighbours, you know, to keep up appearances. They all had to be given back to their owners. But that's only right, isn't it? I mean, it is right that they should be given back, eh?"

I held her under her arms and kissed her. Behind those wet eyelashes, she was bravely trying to smile.

"Tell me," she insisted, "You're not upset, are you?"

"No, I'm not upset."

"And you won't get upset later?"

"No, I promise."

"Well, you mustn't. You mustn't care about it at all. Forget it; we'll be fine!"

Later, one by one, the bed, all the cloth, the dresses, the carpet, the kilims, and then my navy suit, tie and shoes all went back to their owners. My wife laughed out loud at the fact that even the clothes I had worn were someone else's.

"Don't worry darling," she said, "we might not have much, but at least we have each other, eh?"

So we carried on with our lives, appreciating what we did have.

The End